The Horus Quest

William Shambrook

Order this book online at www.trafford.com
or email orders@trafford.com

Most Trafford titles are also available at major online book retailers.

Note for Librarians: A cataloguing record for this book is available from Library
and Archives Canada at www.collectionscanada.ca/amicus/index-e.html

Printed in Victoria, BC, Canada.

ISBN: 978-1-4120-2940-7 (sc)

*Our mission is to efficiently provide the world's finest, most
comprehensive book publishing service, enabling every author to
experience success. To find out how to publish your book, your way, and
have it available worldwide, visit us online at www.trafford.com*

Trafford rev. 9/17/2009

 www.trafford.com

North America & international
toll-free: 1 888 232 4444 (USA & Canada)
phone: 250 383 6864 ♦ fax: 812 355 4082

The Horus Quest By William Shambrook.

Chap 1

If I could choose an adventure, I would never have chosen this one. I don't know exactly how it started, but the trouble I found myself in was frightening. All I had wanted was to realise a boyhood ambition to explore the ancient Egyptian temples that had fascinated me throughout my life.

The crowd had formed like a phantom all around me. It had crept like the falling of night. I suppose I had been too preoccupied in my enthusiasm to experience all I could in the two short weeks allowed by the package holiday, to even notice the increase of humanity at such a deserted spot.

I tried not to panic and looked around for my taxi driver who had left me at this isolated temple. He would most probably reassure me that my fears were silly and that the crowd was just a bit curious. The taxi had gone! I had been abandoned to fend for myself.

A tall mean looking, cadaverous individual wearing a small white turban and attired in a pale blue galabia that hung like a loose dress, stepped forward and approached me. Thoughts of trying to

run or bluff my way out of it ran panic like through
my balding sunburnt head.

Two cohorts of his also approached either side of
him; they shuffled towards me. Little children
coursed like terriers around their ankles, stirring up
the fine sand into a miniature lunar landscape and
cutting off my only escape from this silent temple.
The stark sunshine now turned my eyes into almost
useless shuttered organs restricting my vision and
enhanced the fear I now felt. What a fool I had been
to go off the safe conducted tours and try to make
my own way. I now regretted my impetuosity and
obvious lack of local knowledge. In all this time the
only sound was like the scurrying of rats over a
rocky surface, how silent it really had been. The
sand had devoured the noise and the sun had
blinded my eyes to all but the murals I had been
examining. I noticed now how long the shadows
were becoming and how large his now was.

'Effendi' His voice was a surprise, I had expected a
grating snarling sound but he was like water
cascading downhill, quiet and refined.

'Yes' I said, trying to mask any of my fear and at the
same time drawing myself up to my full height,
attempting to intimidate him.

'What can I do for you?' I said, hoping that this
person only wanted a little baksheesh.

'Are you the man who gave these to our children?'
He asked, thrusting a cheap ballpoint pen at me.
Calamitous thoughts entered my brain at the speed
of an express. Had a child choked on one? Had
some child died or been injured by one? Should I
deny everything and try to make my way out of
here? 'Why do you want to know?'
'Your gifts are not normal. No tourist gives pens to
more than twenty children. We feel that you may be
the person to help us. We feel that you might care
enough to help. You clearly care about us and not
just our monuments.' Whilst saying this, his spindly
arms were moving to point to the urchins who were
now grinning at me and then to the pillars of the
temple.
'If you want some more I shall be most pleased to
let you have them,' I said with genuine passion.
A feeling of profound relief rolled over me. This
was not a menacing crowd but a grateful one. They
did not know that a friend of mine had told me that
pens were important to the youngsters who could
not afford them locally. I had bought a very large
box and taken it with me on this holiday to placate
the crowds of children I had been told to expect at
the various archaeological sites.
'Any more would be good,' he said quietly. 'Would
you be my guest and come to my house?' I would
like to talk with you.'

Not knowing where my taxi was, or if my refusal would offend, I felt the need to think this one out. Also not being in a position of strength and having heard rumours of tourists who disappear, and being within a mile of a site where four foreign tourists were killed last year I did not feel it prudent to antagonise him. My thoughts were thus influenced more by caution than logic.

'I would like that very much.' I said. Not wanting to be rude or unreasonable.

I might after all find out a little of the local culture and possibly be able to add to my after dinner anecdotes at least. My curiosity, now having started to take over my initial fear and surprise, was allowing me a little enjoyment.

He turned and in so doing said, 'Kindly follow me'. So preceded by a horde of children plus a few skinny adults, we made our way through an adjacent palm grove towards a dusty village huddled softly among the featureless dunes.

I was aware of the eyes that watched me from the many impoverished doorways and side streets strewn with rubbish, more little smiling children, palm leaves and animals.

The outward poverty shouted from the mud brick walls and crumbling buildings that appeared to be either growing out of, or falling into the bleached dust that formed the ground over which I now walked. I was aware of the stark contrast between the earth and sky. Cheap trinkets, tee shirts and statues poked out of every hovel that wanted to call itself a shop. The grit was rubbing my sunburned neck and was being washed by my sweat, down to my waistband and I could feel the small of my back was sopping wet beneath my shirt. My camera strap wanted to embed itself into my right shoulder and my knapsack only increased the wetness problems where it touched my shirt.

My shadow danced in front of me like a black pool as its lines enveloped the various contours of the path. It was as though the heat was causing it to stick as well.

My guide simply moved with no apparent problems, at a pace that made me breathless. His sandals seemed to dance over the ground hardly raising the dust.

'It is not far now, just along here.' He said, raising his arm and indicating a tarmac road that ran like a black river in front of us. We turned right and into a little square formed by a few larger buildings that huddled together and nestled into the sloping hillside.

Once there, I followed him into the open doorway of a mud brick house two stories high with a woven straw mat on stilts that seemed to serve as a roof.

Its exterior walls were whitewashed and decorated
with childish pictures lacking in perspective, the
sort a seven-year old might draw. There were
aeroplanes and sphinxes arrayed with camels and
cobras. A sign also crudely drawn said J. Fayed
Antiquities. I smiled inwardly at this attempt at
commerce. He turned to me and said most humbly
'Welcome to my home. Do come in'.
As I followed him through the gaily-painted
doorway he spoke in his native tongue to a child
waiting there, it scurried off into the heavily shaded
rear of the house.
We entered, and the enveloping shadow was like a
fridge door about my back as it clamped the heat
along with the light. I was ushered into a doorway
on my right.
'Please sit down' he said, I looked around, my eyes
slowly becoming used to the lack of light and saw a
long cushioned seat which took up one entire wall
that was crudely plastered and painted blue gloss
on which was hung a finely woven carpet.
 To my left I saw a framed photograph of three men
dressed in white stiffly posed smiling at the camera.
I moved closer to see its importance.
 ' That is my father, uncle, and I two years ago, we
are Hajji' he said proudly. 'You would not
understand perhaps?'

I turned to him and replied 'I once worked in Saudi Arabia and my son still does. It is so important for every Muslim to make the journey at least once in their lifetime to the Kaba in Mecca. You must be proud to have gone together as a family'
 I was thinking how did such an apparently poor family afford to go on such an expensive journey? Or was it a subsidised thing? Their present circumstances gave every indication of a lack of money. This was beginning to be a little more than I had first expected. He smiled at me and beckoned me to sit down. This I did.
A rustling noise to my right announced a woman wearing the obligatory black robes but with face uncovered. She was carrying a brass long necked teapot and glasses on a heavily engraved brass tray. Her eyes avoided mine as she placed these upon a small three-legged table, which she moved into position with her foot with such precision that the whole motion was silent and smooth.
My host said something to the woman who smiled at me and then withdrew as silently as she had entered. 'We are alone' He said it so quietly that I wondered what the purpose of this whole meeting was. It was stuffy but cosy in the room, shutters outside had barred the sunlight of the day and I now hoped for the cool evening air to filter in.

I waited until he had poured the tea into the glasses and asked 'Is it so important to be alone?'

He replied 'It is so important that no one knows what we say today. Unfortunately others know you are here, many have seen you arrive. I have to ask you for help. I have a problem, which I find so difficult to explain, but first I must tell you my name; it is Jibril. What is your name?'

 I replied.' My name is Francis Edwards and I must say that you have a strange way of making an acquaintance.'

He looked at me, closely examining my face. His was not as fearsome as I had at first thought. In fact it was quite pleasant with a lot of animation and knowledge built into its lined appearance. It was only the light and shade that had played tricks with my fear and surprise.

Pausing for a few seconds, he glanced around as though checking that there was nobody else present and spoke; his voice no more than a whisper.

'I am sorry for that but as you will find out I had no choice, I mean we had no choice.'

'Jibril' I said 'isn't that Gabriel in my language?' I found myself replying at the same volume and felt a bit of an idiot for doing so. 'Can't we speak a bit louder?' I asked.

He nodded his assent and said softly 'The choice is right, you do know our ways, Inshallah, God willing'
I still was perplexed at his behaviour but I knew Egyptians to be a bit melodramatic at times to suit their idea of commerce or odd sense of humour and so I suppose I was not quite prepared for anything else. I decided to play it cool and not to get drawn in to what still possibly could be some form of scam.
I sipped my tea; it was hot and sweet with a touch of wood-smoke and mint. I sat back and let him continue. I did not know that in the telling of his story, from that moment on, my life would never be the same again.

Chap 2

Jibril sat facing me 'It is a long story I hope you will indulge me by not being too impatient. I have waited a long time for you to visit Medinet Habu. I knew you would return there one day'

'I have never been here before in my life' I exclaimed 'this is my first visit to Egypt and definitely my first to the West Bank. You must be confusing me with another person.'

'No Mr Edwards, I have known about you for quite a while now. You are the man I have been expecting, and today when the children described you, I had to bring you here to my home. I understand that you are confused and a bit angry that I am adamant that you are expected.'

'Not angry Jibril, just frustrated that I appear to have lost the plot. I assure you that I have never been here before'

He lifted his hands and smiled. 'Perhaps you were a long time ago but if you will be patient I will try to explain things, but if I knew you were here, then others may too.'

I was really getting a bit inquisitive now. Jibril had mentioned others and also that they knew I was here. Perhaps he meant that I had been in Luxor for a couple of days now. I had not made a secret of my travels. I had not thought it was required. I had not kept a low profile but had enjoyed the friendly banter with most of the traders, cab drivers and itinerant vendors who called out to solicit my custom everywhere I went.

Jibril looked straight at me and lifting his glass, toasted me silently; his eyes, a deep brown, showed deep intelligence.

'It all started about a year ago when a man I knew called Mamout came into my shop to sell me some things. He said that he had a cousin who had found a few artefacts in a hole not far from here. I expected the usual scarab or ushabtiu statue of dubious origin but was surprised when Mamout withdrew a gold ring with an Uchat on it. That is what you might call the eye of Horus Mr Edwards. He also brought a couple of gold necklaces. These things of course cannot be dated precisely except if they are named and so I bought these from him; at a fair price and I did not see him for a while. I supposed that he had no more things; but one evening he brought me an exquisite amulet crafted in gold and some tiny inscribed gold discs around two centimetres in diameter with a hole at the centre also with tiny holes around their circumference. They were joined by a chain, just like a pretty necklace. They were in an ivory coffin shaped box with hieroglyphs and a cartouche, neither, of which I was able to recognise or read.

The workmanship was beyond that of a mere forger and I marvelled at the complexity of it. All of these things were in an outer ebony box of the finest workmanship enamelled so well that it might have been made yesterday. There was a representation of the judgement of Thoth painted on the lid. That is the painting, which shows the weighing of the heart of the dead soul balanced against the feather of truth. Or Maat. Isis is pictured with the Ka or soul. They are looking on as Thoth the ibis headed god with his writing implement in hand examines the balance scales ready to condemn the soul to eternal damnation or eternal life. . Sebek the crocodile-headed god waits to devour the heart should it be the heavier. A soul without a heart was damned indeed Mr Edwards. Another box contained the entire group of boxes, so the entire thing was like a Russian doll, one inside the other. I have no idea why this was'

Jibril turned to me and I realised that I had not even sipped my drink, I looked him in the eyes again, and I suppose I must have shown my ongoing curiosity. To be quite truthful, it was becoming quite a story and I said. 'Please continue, this is very interesting, although I have no idea how I can be of any assistance in this. I am basically an amateur in these matters. My knowledge is superficial to say

the least but I do have some good books back at the
hotel if that might help'
Jibril continued as though he had not heard a word
I had said; his eyes danced in his thin face as he
launched himself into his story. 'Mr. Edwards, I had
never seen such beauty or such a complete set of
ornamental items in all my fifty years. I asked
Mamout where they had been found. He said his
cousin had been working on an extension to the
new access roadway near Howard Carter's house
on the way to the Valley of the Kings not five
kilometres from here and had cut into a small scree
slope to remove loose rock. His hoe had disturbed a
covering stone that had slid aside to reveal a niche,
which concealed a cloth wrapped package that had
appeared very old.
 He had hastily covered it again and had returned
under the cover of darkness to retrieve it. All this
had unnerved him and his family for they were
afraid the department of antiquities would put him
in prison if they found out. He had told no one but
he was unsure if he had been able to recover it
without being seen.
Mamout swore me to secrecy, and because his
family and mine had been doing business for many
generations, he trusted me to keep these things
whilst I examined them more closely. Since the
metal appeared to be gold, I weighed it and we both

noted the reading. He then knew I could not or would not rob him. I promised him that I would give him an answer in two days and he left. I knew the quality of the gold was beyond reproach from my previous purchase of the ring and necklaces and thus felt that I might obtain a reasonable profit from the venture.'

Jibril now became more reflective and I watched his face light up in anticipation of his continuing narrative and felt it to be either a sales pitch for something or one hell of a true story. He continued. 'After my evening prayers I sat down to examine the amulet. The fine workmanship stood out under the lamp on my desk, and armed with a magnifying lens and jewellers-eyepiece, I commenced to examine every detail of this beautiful thing. It was a hawk; its height was about eight centimetres. There was a pin behind the beak and the eyes were of the form of the human. One of the eyes was a hole. The other still had a fragment of jewel in the socket. The jewel was broken into three pieces, but the pieces were still held in place. The feathers were like scales laid into the surface and enamelled in a deep blue. Its feet were clasping something. The light seemed to give it a life of its own and every way I turned it exposed more beauty.

One thing that struck me however, was the precision and attention to the minute detail of the

craftsmanship, which seemed to give this
wonderful thing a radiance, which captivated the
attention of anyone who gazed upon it. It was Mr.
Edwards, the most desirable thing I have ever seen
in my life.

 I had no idea what purpose it served or what use it
had been put to. I could only guess as to why it
existed at all since it was too big for a brooch or a
body worn ornament. I assumed it must have been
made as some form of votive offering or as part of a
shrine or had been removed from something larger
like a crown.

Was there a clue here to its origin and construction?
The day had been long but I scraped off a few tiny
samples of metal to take to a friend for analysis.

I examined the box and was unable to decipher the
writing or markings at all. They were obviously
faked since they were unlike any I had seen in my
entire career. They were certainly not hieroglyphic,
hieretic, or demotic. Those are the three types of
ancient Egyptian writing, as you will already know
Mr Edwards the cartouche, or little box containing
the name of that person who had this beautiful
thing made was clearly inscribed with figures
unknown to me.

The next two days were spent in attempting to
decipher the other characters. There was nothing I
could find to give me even a small clue as to its

pedigree. The metal samples I had taken were
found to be gold of the finest quality. I thus valued
these items as one would simply for the gold
content. I decided that I might keep the box and the
gold discs; which I now assumed to be earrings as
an ornament and to sell the enamelled bird at a
price that would give me a reasonable profit.
You see Mr Edwards, that the government is very
hard on those who sell our countries treasures
illegally. They have spies everywhere and it is thus
very difficult to get the objects out of Egypt.'
'If this is a sales pitch Jibril, and you expect me to
get involved in some illegal activity, I will not be
happy. I was almost beginning to believe your
story'
'No Mr Edwards it is not a sales story. I have no
desire to sell you anything. I just need your help.
Please let me continue and you will then
understand.'
I nodded almost reluctantly also I felt a bit
embarrassed that he might feel I thought he was
lying and I indicated that he continue his narrative.
'Mamout returned that evening and I explained to
him the futility of my research into the items. I told
him of my intention of paying the gold value less
my expenses. This was the best anyone or I could
do in the circumstances without proof that these

were genuine antiquities from a real ancient
Egyptian King.
Mamout agreed that the condition of the box alone
gave the impression that it might have been made
yesterday. I managed to strike a deal with him and
he promised to return with more things his cousin
had found. I paid him what I considered was a fair
sum for what was obviously a clever forgery and
put the items in a safe secret hiding place until I
could dispose of them but circumstances have
changed my plans and I need help.
Now Mr. Edwards what do you think of that?'
'You tell a fine story Jibril. What happened to the
box and all its contents? You said that this was
some time ago. Have you sold it? How can I
possibly help or be of assistance? Also please call
me Francis as we are sharing confidences.'
'Very well Francis; too many questions at the same
time but you are right. I need to bring my story up
to date and so will refresh your palate before I do.'
He rose, took my glass and left the room with the
brass tray and its utensils.
I heard voices raised just enough to make me think
that perhaps he was not quite the master in his own
house
He returned with his wife who was looking
decidedly agitated. She was looking at me with
concern and was obviously a little distressed. He

said. 'You must excuse me Francis. My wife thinks I
have detained you too long as it is dark now and
they may be worrying back at your hotel'
I smiled at her.' I am grateful for your concern but I
am staying at the Joliville which has chalets and
since I am on my own I doubt I will be missed.'
'There, Amina, you see you worry too much.' She
smiled embarrassedly at me and withdrew.
'We must stop for prayers Francis. I shall be a short
while. To keep you occupied however I shall let you
enjoy passing the time with this.' He put an object
in front of me; it was the ebony box.
I felt as though ice-cold water had been poured over
my head, the chill that spread down over my body
froze my whole being. I was speechless. He had not
exaggerated; it was every bit as beautiful as he had
described. In fact it was more so; it was exquisite.
'I will return in half an hour' He left me alone with
the object of his story.
I don't know how long I just gazed at the box. The
picture was precise, without brush marks or any
smearing around the edges, almost as if it was a
photograph. This made me a bit suspicious. It
measured about fifteen centimetres long by eight or
nine. The box stood about ten centimetres high with
what looked to my uneducated eye, hinges made of
gold with a gold clasp to hold the lid shut. The
clasp was shaped in the form of an ankh or the

symbol of life. It fitted into an escapement shaped like an eye or Uchat.

I felt that this item exuded a tangible force; it was screaming out to me that I must possess it. It had to be mine or was it just superstition or the ambience? I had no idea why I wanted it so much but it was not mine. I felt it had taken hold of me and had dug its self into my spirit. This made me feel a bit stupid.

Here was I sitting in a little house on the west bank of the Nile with a potential archaeological find which would stand on a level with some of the best discoveries in the last seventy-five years or so since Howard Carter opened the treasury of Tutankhamen. Why me? Or I suppose, why not me? What the hell was I getting into?

I picked the precious object up and turned it to the light so I might better see the surface finish. It was like glass. How on earth could they have made this wonderful thing thousands of years ago? It had to be faked.

Jibril returned as I turned it slowly. He stood silently observing my gyrations of the box. 'I too have done that. What do you think?' He said.

'I need more time I am not an expert in these matters. I simply have no idea what to say or really think' I replied.

'Time is not what we have.' He said gravely. 'At the mosque I have just learned that both Mamout and his cousin have just been found. They had been terribly tortured and murdered. I have returned quickly to help you get away from here. The killers were obviously looking for these things.' I gasped. As I looked at him, the wonderful feeling I had been experiencing, evaporated so fast I could almost see the steam.

I now found myself in a bit of a fix. I was undecided as to how far my involvement in this matter would put me in danger. What had started, as an interesting aside to a holiday excursion only a few hours ago, to soak up the ambience, had now turned decidedly nasty.

I really was in no position to get involved at all. I was out of my depth and certainly out of my league. I did not speak the language and would stand out like a sore thumb in European clothes at a local market. I felt unsure of what exactly I could do in the circumstances other than to get the hell out of here. But why involve me any way?

'Jibril, what the hell has this got to do with me? I sympathise but how can I be of assistance here?'

'Francis, only you can help us. All things will become clear. We have waited for you, or one like you but I cannot tell you now. I do not have the time and neither do you'

I was surprised that he would have chosen me at all
as I am certainly not the "James Bond" type of
person neither in temperament or looks.

I am 44 years old, brown eyed, dark haired, about
five foot ten, slightly overweight, with a ready
laugh and I work as an engineer.

Because I possess a better than average diagnostic
ability I have travelled around the world a lot,
working on several continents. This has always
made me see more to life than the superficial
surface others seem satisfied with. I love to think
things through and plan my moves carefully. A
sense of reason, coupled with a Catholic upbringing
and an early instilled fear of God, had moderated
my entire life to date, and I suppose, formed my
character to be both open and trusting, with a very
ingrained set of values.

Having once served in Her Majesties Armed Forces
in the Royal Engineers defusing bombs and
blowing up useless ordinance all over the place, I
had no illusions or hang-ups, in fact it had given me
confidence and the ability to look after myself.

I was married once, a long time ago at the age of
eighteen out of necessity, at that time we were two
teenagers playing at being adults; a military wife
who followed my career and who eventually found
another in alcohol. The experience left me shattered
and disillusioned with love and the false sense of

security it gives to the one who loves truly. I was however; left alone with my son, Steven, now twenty-six who now worked on contract in Saudi Arabia and around the Middle East on various construction-projects. He thinks of me as a brother and I love him most dearly. He was the only consolation to a severe misuse of ten years of my life His was the only photo I carried.

It had been at his suggestion a few weeks ago during one of his rare telephone calls home that I should take a break from my work.

I had now taken two weeks out of a busy schedule to fulfil my dream of walking amongst the temples of a civilisation that I had fantasised about for as long as I can remember. 'Dad' he had said, 'You need some adventure in your life, get out more and live a little' How true I now thought, but if this is living then I'm not sure that it's for me. However I had followed his suggestion of an Egyptian vacation; then gone to the travel agent and booked this holiday.

I brought myself to bear on my predicament. This could get quite nasty, as I had no idea what I was getting myself into; let alone the consequences of coming into contact with the people who had erased Mamout and co. Logic alone should drive me away from this place but there were other dangers and difficulties that my being here would heap upon me, and soon too by the look of it.

My reasoning now told me that there could be a problem with my presence having been noted by the entire village and that anyone searching for any extraordinary occurrence or clue would be led right to Jibril's front door. I reasoned that I should bow out now and try to get a taxi back to my hotel. Where was I likely to find one out here though? I had not seen a car since I came into this village.

Perhaps though, that might not be a good idea either as taxis can be traced back to both ends of a journey. I did not want to advertise where I had come from. It was still possible to slip away and hide amongst the other tourists. It was also probable that whatever I did, it would not disassociate me from the presence of these treasures. I too would be a target for whoever was out to get them. I was involved whether I liked it or not.

I would thus have to engage in some sort of damage limiting exercise and get the hell out of here without being seen or caught. I felt that this was getting a bit ridiculous and perhaps I might be overreacting. But was I?

Apart from its value, the box was beautiful, was it enough to kill two men for? Was I also going to be a victim?

Chap 3

'You must go, get away from here Francis'. Jibril grasped my hand. 'I give you this. Take it with you. He thrust the box at me. ' I can't take this' I blurted. 'You will understand soon enough Francis. You cannot refuse to take it; did you not feel it reach out to you? Do you not desire to have it?' I nodded, reluctantly took it and stuffed it into my knapsack. 'I will say I sold it some time ago. You must not fail me. Make use of what it will teach you. Please go now. I will try to contact you if I can. Until then, you must save these things. Do not let our enemies gain possession of this box and its secrets. There is no time to explain, but this has always been yours. I promise you that you will know what to do. It has already talked to you. I saw it in your face when I returned. I am only returning it to you for now is the time. It has always been so. Now barra, outside' So saying, he guided me out into a small rear courtyard. I was aware now that night had fallen and the local lighting was somewhat ineffectual. 'Climb over the wall here and hide in the temple. May Allah protect you.' His pleading face reflected enough moonlight to convince me he was in earnest and that I should not delay. 'May he protect you too' I said as I dropped into a rubbish-filled alley and stumbled away.

I could not go to any of the new hotels situated
nearby, as whoever was after the boxes would be
able to spot me. Also I had an illegal object in my
knapsack, I couldn't even ask a policeman for help.
I was on my own and needed to think and
consolidate whatever advantages I had.

I should hide up and get some idea who my
prospective pursuers were. Failure to do this now
could be the death of me. It was possible that I
might run into them any moment. If they knew me,
then I was already dead. Not a cheering feeling
when you are miles from home and certainly out of
your depth in more ways than one.

I made my way unsteadily due to the unevenness of
the ground which was strewn with small rocks that
in the moonlight were the same colour as the sand,
making them difficult to avoid either kicking,
knocking or just stubbing my toes against.

I could see the temple dimly ahead, stark against
the lighter coloured hills that rose behind it. I only
had a few hundred metres to go. It would offer a
load of hiding places within the several courtyards
and lesser shrines.

Keeping low I crossed a small path and plunged
into an empty irrigation ditch making enough noise
to equal a herd of elephants. Sliding down the side,
I cursed as I grazed my arm on an Aloe Vera plant,
which flicked and cut me below my right eye I

could feel the blood warm upon my cheek. I ended
my impromptu journey on my back and smothered
in dust. Climbing back out I could not help thinking
what the hell was I doing? I began dusting myself
off just in case I had picked up some insect like a
scorpion or spider, panting as I did so.

A snuffling growling noise distracted me from my
pain and I saw a cur of a dog slope off into a small
palm grove about twenty metres to my left. No
danger there I thought but I had better get going
away from the path. It would be too obvious a route
for any pursuit so I must hide pretty soon or be
caught in the open.

One thing was in my favour. I had done my
homework. I knew quite a lot about the temple I
was about to stumble into. I had spent the day there
before Jibril had enticed me into this gamut of
emotions, this adventure; I had also researched its
history because the king who created it had
fascinated me.

Ramesses III had built it during his long reign and
had called it 'His mansion of millions of years.
United with eternity in the estate of Amon.' I knew
it as Medinet Habu. He had actually lived there
with his family during the XX dynasty around 1200
years BC. It was basically a sandstone and granite
temple set around with massive mud brick walls,
some of which had crumbled back to dust.

I must say at this juncture that I am not the hero
type. Discretion to me certainly is the better part of
valour and absence of body beats presence of mind
any time. I have had my scraps and scrapes during
my youth and had enjoyed my interesting military
career in bomb disposal and ordinance but at nearly
forty-five, I thought they were behind me. I had
chosen to explore and understand the wonders of
my past. Now I found myself possibly sought by
merciless torturers and killers whilst I held in my
possession an object that was to my pursuers,
certainly more valuable than my life. I had to find a
safe place to hide and fast.

I approached the small ancient gatehouses that
straddled the only entrance on the eastern side and
slipped through the low chain-link modern fence
that hung from uprooted iron bars.

 If only I could have gone east to the Nile and back
to my hotel I thought; but I would not have been
able to make the eight-kilometre journey unseen.
This would have to do, as unprepared as I now was.
I was also very unsure whether I could involve
anyone else without placing him or her or myself in
more danger.

Passing between the two once grandiose entrance
pylons on which I could see the giant inscribed
pictures of the king with his club raised as though it
was a tennis racquet illuminated by the moonlight. I

climbed a small staircase cut into the stone on my right that at one time would have led to the living quarters all those years ago. I then scaled the broken masonry, climbing up the uneven sides of the pylon, feeling for the slight hand and footholds in the ancient blockwork, my trainers achieving the required grip.

 I then lay panting from the effort, flat on the top of the tower partially concealed by the crumbling cornice. There was no sign of movement but a wailing noise reached me from the direction I had just come. I prayed it was not the unknown persons who were after this object. If it was, then Jibril or his family was the source of the anguish. I trembled, both from the night chill and that thought.

Being in a position of real and I mean genuine danger has the effect of concentrating your senses. I don't mean the pseudo fear of the horror film or the adrenaline rush of the white-knuckle ride or the freefall jump. I mean the primitive fear of being hunted. Once the instinct takes over, an excitement of anticipation hones the senses into a survival mode. The pulse quickens and the muscles are ready to fight or run. The brain kicks in with a precision and providing the sense of reason is not lost within the terror you really feel, then it is possible to control this to your advantage.

I had felt it several times during my career when
confronted with a car bomb or a van filled with
enough fertiliser and diesel fuel to blow the average
street of the face of the earth. I had learned to
recognise the enhancement it had given to my
reason. It would now save me I hoped. At least I
understood my fear and how to use it.

There are good and bad parts to life. We all want
the good parts and tend to ignore the bad,
pretending they do not exist. My previous work
with explosive devices had taught me some very
important facts. Number one; never underestimate
anyone or anything. In other words know your
enemy. This is as important as survival itself even if
you fear him or them. That way you will neither
underestimate him nor overestimate him either. If
some person has made a bomb, then they must
have thought about it. They have gone and
acquired the parts and have assembled a deadly
weapon. It is not like a gun or sword; for you have
to see those you kill.

A bomb is indiscriminate; usually it is a coward's
way to maim, injure or kill people, plus damage
property. A bomb also brings other items like
broken glass and masonry within its blast to kill
more innocents. The simple products of
combustion, carbon dioxide, water and heat when
expended in microseconds have killed more of

mankind than all the plagues, famines and disasters throughout history. No wonder Alfred Nobel felt guilty.

Number two; never think you are cleverer than your enemy. He or she knows that you have to be close in order to defuse his device. He can be miles away; watching you make your approach and could detonate by remote control. He also knows you have to move his creation, so he might fit a trembler switch to kill you, or just anyone who happens to touch. He can set a trap to draw you in. He is the instigator of the hunt and thus can watch as you enter his hunting ground.

Number three; always have enough cynicism to keep looking for a motive. If you don't then you are missing the points of numbers one and two; the bomber intends to create a reaction. You could be dealing with a slab of Semtex -Composition 4 or a chunk of marzipan, while a two tonne bomb is being driven to explode elsewhere. If it is you they are after, the chances are that they will succeed. So know your enemy, or at least believe in him.

My present circumstances did not frighten me; I just could not identify with my antagonists. I just had not had sufficient time to get used to the events that had put me in this situation. I felt that I knew their motives but recognising the persons was going to be difficult. I realised that the other problem I had

was that I could not communicate with anyone else
I knew I could trust.
 Of course I could go back to the village but Jibril
was unable to help me any more than he had
already. I would just have to wait and hide to see
the night through, or at least get some idea of the
trouble I could see I was in. The dogs were barking
in the distance. I was amazed how clearly the sound
travelled over the cool sand. It made me aware also
that there was a faint sound of a car approaching.
 I turned onto my side and looked back towards the
houses that stood about half a kilometre away.
Light from a few naked bulbs cast long shadows
out into the desert. I saw headlights sweep the
buildings; I knew that they were coming for me. I
should have gone north towards the hotels but that
was where they would be looking for me. It would
be easy for them to just watch the little road that led
there. Perhaps that was what they had been doing
already. I still did not have any idea how many of
them would be involved or how well organised
they were. Only time would tell. I was better off
here where I could spot whoever might be coming
after me or at least try.
Feeling in my multi-zipped pocketed trousers, I
could not find a weapon, even a penknife or
screwdriver would have been useful. I explored my
knapsack and ran my fingers over the box.

As the moon rose higher in the starry canopy I was able to see Orion rising with such clarity above me. Because of the clear desert air and the lack of reflected light; I being new to Egypt had not realised before that the stars were so bright. I now understood the impact of such a night sky on the ancients who had constructed this wonderful temple on top of which I now lay. It was as though all I had to do was reach out to touch the brilliant points of light that seemed to rest in their dark soft foam above me.

 I watched the rotation of the heavens, just perceptible as the minutes passed away. The sheer panorama of the night sky calmed my fear momentarily. Jupiter scraped above the horizon, a white light added to the many.

A noise below, I rolled over looking down and saw two shadowy figures creep along the path I had crossed. They were well illuminated by the silvery light. A small quantity of high cloud slipped in front of the moon casting a deep grey shadow. I could not follow their movements any longer. A crashing, then a ripping sound, a series of curses, I then knew someone had taken the same route as I, down into the ditch. A further scraping noise told me they were at the entrance. Muffled voices drifted up to me and I caught a few words of what I thought was English being spoken. I strained my ears to gather whatever information I could. The words kill and bastard confirmed my suspicions. It was English, well American actually, and it was me they wanted.

They were close; I could smell stale tobacco and cheap after-shave. I prayed they could not smell my fear. Keeping as low as possible I gently, oh so gently moved my head to see what they were doing. They were now directly beneath me on the stairs that entered the right hand pylon. Even if they crossed the walkway between the left and right pylons they would not see me unless they too climbed up the nearly sheer sides. I made up my mind to sacrilegiously remove a piece of cornice and throw it down on anybody who might make the attempt. Until then however I would lie here between prehistory and the stars.

Pharaohs had walked these walls. Perhaps they had thought as I was doing now. I could not believe that I was as relaxed as this when at least two killers were after my blood. Was I going mad? Was this a dream or not? Any moment now I would wake up and get ready for work. I could hear the beating of my heart and feel a small stone pressing into the base of my spine. I could see the night sky as though it was a planetarium. So unless the roof had blown off my bedroom, I was wide-awake!

A little time passed, the moon pushed her light out again from under the soft cloudy curtain. My two pursuers moved more noisily and I watched them starkly illuminated in the silver glow. Dark corridors picked out in shadow lay around them. I wondered how long they would look for me.

The two men really were making a lot of noise now and would have caught me had I stayed on the ground. They flitted in and out of the many pillars and seemed to be covering most of the courtyards extremely quickly; I wondered how they had chosen to look here. Had I left a trail? Perhaps they were simply thinking that I had to do the obvious thing and come here.

The second chamber they were searching contained the defaced statues of Ramesses Behind these square based pillars, carved on the walls were the numerous pictures of his conquests. I had been examining them when Jibril had made my acquaintance just a few hours ago. During his long reign, Ramesses had instigated a bonus scheme to his troops as they had defeated the various tribes to the north. For every right hand cut off the stricken enemy soldiers, he had paid a premium. There were shown graphically as piles of hands with scribes noting their numbers.

A fraud had soon developed amongst his obviously greedy troops. They inserted the left hands of the slain as well as those of the female camp followers. The pictures then showed Ramesses and his solution. The premium would only now be paid for the genitalia as well. This horrific solution was obvious by the large piles of male organs also being counted by the scribes carved in bas-relief in the temple walls.

 The invading Libyans had been annihilated and castrated. As if it was bad enough to lose. Perhaps they were not dead when some mad Egyptian soldier hacked off their testicles with a blunt bronze blade shaped like a scythe. At least that explained the sword's shape anyway I thought.

Obviously old Ramesses had been quite a nasty fellow. He clearly had little regard for those who stood in his way. There were at this moment like-minded persons down there with the same ethos, who would certainly cut me off in my prime should I be discovered. I also recalled that it was not too far from where I lay that Ramesses had succumbed to a mysterious illness less than a month after a failed insurrection. Poisoned perhaps by his son or one of the priesthood, nevertheless it was a sobering thought. Whatever my possible future was to be; I really did not want to be united with eternity quite yet.

Chap 4

As I lay there contemplating my imminent fate, there came a yelp out on the road. The dog I had seen earlier had found something that had startled it. A rat or scorpion perhaps? It was certainly to my advantage as the two villains drew pistols that caught the moonlight and then ran crouched low, back towards the entrance seeking cover from one another. They separated and made their way back through the wire fence in an attempt to encircle whatever or whomever they had thought made the noise, namely me. One of them attempting an encircling route promptly fell into a continuation of the original ditch. His weapon fired with the intensity of what seemed to be an atom bomb in the stillness, and in its muzzle flash I saw part of his head explode. The bloody fool had shot himself. His partner thinking that he too was under fire let off nearly a full magazine of nine millimetre automatic rounds in the general direction of his stricken companion. I could see the flashes, which lit up the giant walls like some evil son e Lumiere. At the same time, the crashing explosions of the shots were bouncing off the nearby cliffs and returning delayed by distance, to add to the terrific commotion which would bring the entire population here, or perhaps keep them all away.

I was surprised that I could also hear the self-cocking action of the large handgun and the gentle tinkle of the brass cartridge cases hitting the ground amongst the fusillade. I thanked all that was holy for my relatively safe position away from this inept and dangerous exchange of fire providing none of the erratic shots came my way.

As I was so engaged, a return shot from the ditch where the first man had fallen; caught the hitherto unscathed villain full square in the throat, the heavy bullet whipping his head violently backwards and sending his body into spasm. His arms shot out as though he was being crucified, the gun flying from his hand clattering along the entrance steps not far below me. He now brought both hands to his mortally wounded neck and with frenzy attempted to stem the jugular flow that was like a stygian river running down his clothing. In the moonlight it looked like a living, glistening snake exiting from his head.

A gurgling scream lifted its way to me. I felt absolutely no emotion or empathy for these tragic events that seemed to be played out for my amusement. He fell over and a dark sinister lake formed quickly around him. He moaned, like the last gurgles of a bagpipe and was still.

What had happened? The answer was not long in coming as his badly injured partner crawled over

the lip of the ditch, gun in hand. Leaving quite a
trail of blood, he proceeded to make his painful way
towards his now obviously dead companion.

His face half devoured by the blast of his own
weapon was evil, like some monster from the
depths of Hell. Perhaps he was still unaware of his
mistake in shooting his partner because upon
reaching him and turning the body over he let out
an awful inhuman wail which was beyond the
experience of man to hear, or for me to ever recall,
without turning my blood to ice. As he looked up in
his anguish I was presented with a view of his face,
so horrible due to the jaw having been blown away
and hanging by gooey muscular tissue down the
front of his collar. His right eye had gone and the
blackness of the empty socket looked like a gateway
to his inner hell He was hideous.

The moonlight that illuminated his travesty of a
face was from behind me, so he was looking into
the light and could not see me. Just to be sure I kept
absolutely still and not draw his attention via his
one remaining eye.

I wondered how much longer he could endure the
loss of blood and the obvious pain the terrible
wound must be inflicting. He began to run round in
circles, screeching, jabbering and banging into
chunks of broken masonry. Falling time and time
again, he would drag himself up and wave his

pistol at the moon. At last, raising the weapon to his forehead he ended the misery of his intolerable agony. The crash of the pistol, the crunching noises as he fell and the ensuing silence were a welcome finale to us both. I could not feel sorry, only relief because he had received the evil fate that he had obviously desired for me.

Climbing down was difficult because I was shaking with that relief, fear, cold and tiredness which comes after threat. I leapt the final few feet and made my way over to the dead assailants. I had to find out who they were, and what it was they really wanted, also the reason for such heavy-handed methods. I still had no idea who they were working for or how much they really had known.

It would not have been much use to me if my involvement had been broadcast all over the place since they could get me any time they wanted. They had been looking for me, hadn't they?

I did not know how much time I had before the local police or the inhabitants of the nearby hotels would investigate the fusillade of shots. It had been like Guy Fawkes Night or a rowdy New Years Eve celebration.

Quickly and unwillingly I searched the bloody pockets of both men. I extracted wallets and any papers I could find making sure I left no fingerprints by using a piece of carrier bag I had found attached to the chain-link fence nearby. My stomach turned, as I could not help looking into the shattered face of what once had been a living, breathing person; it brought back some of the pulped faces I had seen during my career. I was not unaffected even now; I had never lost my humanity.

Leaving the money I found, I only took papers and returned both wallets into their respective pockets and having found a smaller automatic pistol on one of them, I took that as well. It was best to leave as little information for the ensuing police investigation. I had to get out of here. They must have heard this fracas in Luxor and that was six or more Kilometres away.

By now the moon was descending and its shadows were lengthening again. I retraced my steps and so passed by the hidden ditch that had been both trap and salvation for me. Glancing down I saw a glint of reflected moonlight cast back by something. Going down properly this time and without incident, I saw that it was an attaché case, black, with chrome bindings. It was these that had reflected the light. I tried the two catches. The damn thing was locked; I would have to go back to find the key.

I thought I heard voices and vehicles starting up about half a kilometre over to my left. It was obviously an investigating party. It had surprised me how quickly the entire horrific episode had taken place. I knew that if I did not move off South down the road in the next few moments that I would be seen.

 Picking up the briefcase I ran keeping low and attempting to put as much distance between the gory scene and myself I left the same way I had entered. Taking the easy route and not wanting to leave a trail in the sand, I used the small paved roadway that meandered along to the low hills that formed the boundary to this valley. There were other villages to my left. I would have to pass them if I were to get away. I hoped that there was nobody to see me here but that had to be impossible since everybody living around here would have had an early morning wakeup call courtesy of Smith and Wesson and the shootout at Medinet Habu. Damn! I was in the middle of the proverbial creek in a barbed wire canoe. It was not getting any easier either. I was not as fit as I used to be and certainly unprepared for this situation.

Reasoning that the pursuit would come once everyone had investigated where the noise had come from, it was logical just for me to get away with the minimum of fuss and escape detection by being invisible. I just had to run as fast as possible and put distance between me and the source of the commotion. Soon I was dragging myself along, I had a stitch in my right side and my lungs were incapable of extracting any more oxygen. My knapsack straps rubbed my shoulders and the briefcase kept banging my thigh.

I felt something was wrong, I wasn't sure. Gasping, I threw myself into a clump of reeds. Just in time, an army vehicle travelling without lights came around the bend in front of me. The great solid wheels thrumming a low-pitched note on the thin tarmac. But for my involuntary action, they would have seen me. I had not heard its approach due to the noise of my breathing and the rushing sound of my elevated blood flow in my ears. I would have to be more careful.

I lay there; breathing slowly as I waited until my fear and fatigue had diminished somewhat. The sound of shouting and engines reached me from the Temple and I could see headlights reflected off the pylon that I had lain upon. I had come about two kilometres. I would have to go further but there was no sign of pursuit, so perhaps those investigating the killings were not looking for me yet.

With a tinge of gold in the eastern sky the new day began. I raised myself and started back towards the Nile. I couldn't get lost provided I went towards the dawn. I would have to be extremely careful as there was so little cover and with the coming light it would be easy to spot a solitary figure moving down the valley.

I had to get back to my hotel. I needed to escape. I needed time to think and recuperate. I needed a shower. I wondered if they were looking for me in particular. It would be sensible to divest myself of this briefcase as it might betray me.

Stopping near a clump of papyrus reeds and ragged palm trees that marked a waterhole I slid down its side and, with my feet standing in the turgid green water, I extracted a stone and promptly commenced to demolish the locks. After about two minutes of battering, interspersed with pauses to check I had not alerted any pursuers, I achieved success. The case fell open.

Inside was a large quantity of money in the form of dollar bills. The smallest of which was a hundred. It was a very thick wad. I could just make things out in the lightening dawn. There were some papers, another gun, some photographs, and two passports. I stuffed the money into my knapsack and. I hid the gun, in a small hole in the bank removing the rounds and the magazine lest a child find it. The papers and photographs were stuffed down my by now very dusty tee shirt. I must now move on, it was not wise to stay any longer. I turned the case and examined it once more just perhaps I had missed something.

There was a slight discrepancy in the depth of the inside with respect to the outside. It had a false bottom. Losing patience, I tore at the base, which came away reluctantly to reveal two very slim boxes. Damn, I would have to find space for these too .in my sack.

Sinking the case by stamping it into the water, I pulled down a few stones to keep it submerged and climbed up out of the waterhole. Carefully rearranging the foliage to minimise the risk of discovery, I scuffed my wet trainers in the sand to remove any tracks. I would try the bridge over the Nile, which I had seen from my hotel. Perhaps I might cross it hidden amongst the mass of humanity on its way to work in Luxor.

On I went, crossing the remaining distance diagonally, skirting the irrigation ditches and villages, trying not to disturb the inevitable dogs too much. I did not want to be seen. I did not dare to think what the authorities would think of my escapade back at the temple.

There was no way that I could explain the previous night's events. I could not even believe the story myself. How then could I defend myself from the inevitable charges of robbery, murder and the theft of ancient artefacts plus the documents and money? The sky was now perceptibly lighter and down on my left I was able to see the Colossi of Memnon sitting facing the rising of the sun as these giant statues had done for millennia. They were reputed to sing in the early dawn as the warming rays, heated the stone. Tourists would start the tour here, prior to visiting the Valley of the Kings, before the burning heat of the day developed.

 The desert floor was becoming visible by the second as the sun poked its tendrils of gold into the early morning mist; it is an amazing thing that there is a definite border between the cultivated land and the desert. The foliage stands as though pruned into a straight line with no intermediate mixing. It is either in the land of the living or the land of the dead. It was along this green grey boundary that I made my way carefully towards the rising sun.

 To my left, the muted sound of a hot air balloon burner drew my gaze towards the Theban cliffs; I looked at the multicoloured globe as it rose majestically into the still, clear, chill desert air. I wished that I were aboard to take in the beauty of a bird's eye view. Too many people were about. It was getting too busy to hide; I could see a tourist bus making its way towards the statues of Memnon.

I changed my plan immediately. I was now too late to make it to the bridge there was too much light. I would certainly be seen now. It was later than I thought. I followed the progress of the bus and

hoped that I could make the distance during its
stop. The bus pulled into the dusty unmade area at
the edge of the road that served as a car park, and
disgorged its obligatory tourists. If I could just go
about half a kilometre, I would join them and
hopefully hide myself amongst them. I needed to
rest and where better than inside this air-
conditioned luxury leviathan?

 I started to make my way back, along the road that
had led me into this adventure. I was wary that as
few persons as possible should see me. I did not
want any pointing fingers now. Thankfully, I
thought, those locals present were more interested
in parting the visitors from their money than in
observing another traveller arriving, as dusty and
dishevelled as me.

I was able to approach from behind some straggling
palm trees and a clump of papyrus that was
growing in a defunct irrigation ditch not far from
the bus. The chatter of humanity posing for the
inevitable photo, mixed with the low beat the diesel
engine of the coach was making to maintain the air
conditioning, masked any noise I made in the final
few yards of my approach. It also brought my
senses back to the normality I needed to re enter the
company of others.

The crowd had its back to me as I edged forward as
if to lose myself within its sense of security. I felt a

strong desire that I had to get to sleep as well; my body was tired and I was still running on adrenalin but the gauge said empty. Nobody was looking at me I hoped.

I really prayed that there were going to be no embarrassing questions to answer for my weird arrival.

Chap 5

I slipped in behind the group and was really glad to recognise several faces I had seen at my hotel. This was going to be a little easier than I had thought. I had actually booked on this tour. I would have been here anyway. What with all the mayhem of the last night, I had forgotten all about it. What luck, but how to explain my absence from its start? Especially looking, as scruffy and dirty as I must do now.

I listened to the guide telling about the statues of Ramesses the great. 'These were erected about 1250 BC and were damaged by an earthquake. The contraction and expansion of the stone made a noise like singing sometimes.'

The guide having finished his story, now noticed me and came over saying, 'where have you been'? I mumbled something like 'I overslept and got on the wrong bus.' I could see he was looking at my dusty clothes so I added 'And I fell into a hole on the way here' I was not sure he believed me.

'Can you help me tidy up?' I asked whilst waving a large denomination note in front of his face.

He was extremely pleased to find me a baseball cap and a change of tee shirt, which he bought from an itinerant vendor who was slightly less scruffy than I was. I tipped him handsomely for his efforts and conspiratorially said I had woman trouble and

would he not mention this sad occurrence. He
grinned widely and nodded his assent.

No wonder; I had just given him three months
salary.

I now retreated into the coach and changed quickly
at the rear. The chill of the air-conditioning went
right through to my bones. I then went outside and
bought two bottles of water.

 The first I drank without even stopping to breathe.
The second I took with me behind the coach. There,
out of sight of my travelling companions and the
locals,

I performed rudimentary ablutions on my armpits,
as not to offend their olfactory senses when they
had to join me on the bus. I felt that I must smell
like a polecat after a night on the tiles.

 I poured the remainder over my head, wiping my
face and hands in my soiled shirt from last night.
I looked at myself in the driving mirror and was
amazed at the two-minute transformation:

 I now at least looked almost human. Apart from
needing a shave and the reddening scratch below
my right eye, I was almost presentable.

 I then made sure the bits and pieces I had collected
on my night journey were safely put into my
knapsack. Joining the tour in its last few minutes I
was assailed by the inevitable hawkers and
vendors. I bought some obvious tat and a selection

of papyrus pictures. I was even beginning to enjoy
the bargaining banter.

One item was a soapstone model of a falcon, which
seemed quite beautifully, made. There was an
ushabtiu statue of Tutankhamen style made of
wood, which had been finely polished. It stood on a
box- like base.

I haggled until it was time to go and was able to
extract the last vestige of discount from the vendor
as the coach started to move. I then wrapped the
items I had collected in my old shirt and tied the
package with the sleeves and stuffed it into the top
of my knapsack, which was by now bulging, but it
would serve to hide the items within.

. Amid the tut tuts from my new companions who
had been kept waiting, I made my way to the back
of the coach carrying my latest acquisitions.

The tour was to Deir al Bahari, from whence I had
seen the balloon rise earlier, first stopping at the
temple of Queen Hatshepsut or Maatkara. It had
always impressed me because it uses a curve in the
giant golden sandstone cliff to act as a majestic
natural backdrop to a style so modern and
sympathetic with the environment. I listened as our
guide described the building of this beautiful
temple.

The greatest architect of that time, Semut had built
three terraces leading up to the vertical cliff face

and had added pillars, which still bore the Colours originally painted on them. Hatshepsut had married her half brother Thothmes II and had kept the throne when he died and because of her forceful character, had ruled as co-regent for twenty-one more years with her nephew Thothmes III. Because of her great skill in government she was allowed to reign supreme, contrary to ancient tradition. The paintings on her very modern looking temple show an expedition to the land of Punt which some think may be Zimbabwe. Her tomb had never been found. Because, as a woman, she had not been allowed to be buried in the Valley of the Kings. There had been chauvinism in those days as well. We all shuffled around the monument and I enjoyed the normality. I suppose I was unwinding from the problems of the night before. I could speak several languages, basically because I am a bit of a mimic and have a prodigious memory for detail. It had helped me learn to read a lot of the hieroglyphics on the temple walls. In fact I had found it surprisingly more than easy. That was why I soon found myself absorbed in the writing on the walls and pillars.

I had never questioned this ability; it was just simple to me. I suddenly realised I had no need to refer to the guidebook I had bought to know what everything meant; now that was odd, I was sure I could not have done this yesterday.

Somehow I had cracked it, but I supposed that if others could do it, so could I.   After a few minutes however I found that I could not concentrate on the present. My thoughts were being dragged backwards. I felt that it must be because I was tired.

I could not drive it all from my mind and put it into perspective. I had to think but I also had to reason it out.

I kept looking over my shoulder though to see if I was being followed after my escape from Medinet Habu. Surely the police would be out looking for me. I must have left a trail all the way here. I could not even imagine my survival in an Egyptian gaol for even a short time.

I suddenly felt decidedly unwell plus extremely hungry. I went back to the coach; the smiling driver opened the automatic door and I heard the pneumatic hiss as I mounted and was once again enclosed in the air-conditioned haven. I walked to the back and sat down.

I do not remember the rest of the tour as I fell asleep, that deep sleep born of supreme effort and stress. I was awakened by a gentle touch and a sexy voice broke through my limbo state.

'Are you alright?' It said. 'Can I do anything for you? You had better wake up we're back at the hotel.'

I opened my eyes to see a vision, a veritable vision! I did not dare answer lest the breath over my unbrushed teeth offended her.

My mouth felt like the inside of a gerbil cage. The bloody thing was still trying to eat its way out from behind my eyes. They ached like hell. I turned my unshaven face away and replied 'Yes thank you. I had a little accident this morning. I am all right now.' I didn't think she believed a word. 'Can I see you to your room? You have a cut by your eye. Would you like me to fix it for you?' She spoke with real concern and interest. 'Yes thank you' I replied, again turning my breath away I continued. 'I really need a shower and a shave before I can actually face anyone.'

I turned my head back towards her and looked into two of the most beautiful eyes it has ever been my pleasure to encounter. They were soft and reflected the clear blue sky. The vibrancy within them radiated the inner soul of this woman. Her features were classic beauty, well defined. Her skin was tanned but light in colour, her lips were full with a radiant smile that riveted my attention. She really did seem to care, I fell into her gaze and all my anxieties and worries paled into insignificance

beside the overwhelming feelings she was stirring
in my tired and aching body.

She helped me to my feet and led me off the bus
and out into the afternoon sun. I must have looked
drunk to any casual observer. She didn't seem to
mind at all to be associated with me.

We collected our keys from reception where I noted
the occasional raised eyebrow and then went out
towards the swimming pool and its numerous
rainbow patterned sunshades interspersed between
the obligatory thatched poles. The path continued
towards a landing jetty, which was reached by
several tiers of steps. I looked at all my fellow
holidaymakers who were sunning themselves
oblivious to the terror that had lurked so near me
last night.

I noticed that the whole area was covered with
astro-turf. It slightly annoyed me that I had not had
the time to notice it earlier. We now turned right,
past a grinning towel attendant as we made our
way towards our respective chalets between hedges
of bougainvillaea, frangipani and lotus.

I walked slightly behind her, enjoying the gentle
swaying of her slim body and the fragrance of the
beautiful gardens. Her chestnut hair cascaded
around her shoulders, stirring in the Nile breeze.

'I must seem extremely rude' I said, 'My name is
Francis, Francis Edwards, amateur Egyptologist

and Engineer, not necessarily in that order.' She
stopped and turned towards me. It was all I could
do not to hug her to me. God what was happening
to me? I inwardly told myself to stop acting like an
adolescent schoolboy and to control my lascivious
inner self. 'Pleased to meet you Francis. My name is
Anna Scarletti. I am a doctor of astronomy' I
laughed and said, 'When I awoke I thought you
were an angel. No wonder you have such a caring
manner.' She replied with a laugh 'you looked so
lonely and unwanted back there in the coach, that I
had to do something. I knew from the last few days
that you were on your own.' Then almost
suspiciously she added. 'I am surprised I did not
notice you when we set off this morning'.
I let it ride but I remembered now, I too had noticed
her a couple of days ago, sitting all by herself at the
evening buffet meal on my first day. I too had sat
alone; not wanting to intrude or impose myself on a
lady who perhaps was waiting for someone. Only,
then she had her beautiful hair pulled up tight into
a bun, which had not shown her fine features to
such good advantage. In fact she had looked
austere, like a stern schoolteacher Close up she was
a different individual. I wished that I had seen then,
what I saw now, because perhaps if I had, I would
not have just endured the worst night of my life. It

is easy to regulate ones life with hindsight for it
always has 20:20 vision.

She followed me to my chalet and busied herself
with the air-conditioner, which purred and grunted
into life. 'I will be back in a few minutes,' she said,
sweeping past me, as I stood transfixed on the
threshold. 'Time for you to take that shower.'

Grabbing a fluffy towel from where I had left it to
dry on the patio; I went into the bedroom. I pushed
my old knapsack with its varied contents behind
the mini-bar and entered the bathroom and I was
soon enjoying a solar heated stream of warm water.
The action of scrubbing the dust and dirt of the
night's action away also cleaned my mind and
prepared it for some very clinical thinking.

I really scrubbed my teeth and prepared to shave.
As the steam cleared from the mirror, I could not
believe how much my face had changed. Apart
from the obvious encounter with the Aloe-Vera
bush, I had lost weight and developed quite a
suntan. I lathered up and ran the Bic razor over my
now established stubble. I only cut myself twice,
which for me is an achievement.

A knock on the door announced her return. I
answered it dressed in a towelling robe with two
small patches of toilet tissue still attached to my
face, for in my haste to see her loveliness I had
forgotten them. Fat chance I had of ever making a

good impression. She smiled and said, 'You seem to be eternally in the wars don't you?' I noticed that she too had showered and changed, her still damp hair curling and clinging to her face made her look even sexier. I could see her form silhouetted inside her translucent skirt, by the now late afternoon sun. I invited her in, turning away in my embarrassment, to remove those damn bits of tissue,

Anna sat me down on the edge of the bed and taking a small bottle of hydrogen peroxide and some cotton wool from her bag, proceeded to clean the wound beside my eye. I winced at the pain of the astringent.

She hummed quietly to herself as though she were painting a picture, ignoring my obvious discomfort. 'There you are, Sano e salve as we say in Italy. Safe and sound'. 'Anna, Why did you say that?' I said. 'Francis! Do you think I did not see you join us this morning? You looked as though you had been fighting a war. It is obvious to me that you needed help, and besides you have such lovely eyes.'

'Is that a reason to assist a complete stranger?' I asked. 'It is a good enough reason for me' Said Anna looking at me directly. 'Most people are kind when it really matters.' 'Not the ones I met last night' I said,' I wish I could tell you more but I would not want to involve you in what might turn quite nasty.'

She looked me straight in the eyes and in a low gentle voice, said, 'Sometimes in our lives there are moments when someone reaches out to touch the soul of another. Or perhaps I might say Ka?. It may be you helping me for no reason other than the need to just help. It is I who want to help you for no reason other than the fact you obviously need some assistance, Please do not turn me down.'

To be quite truthful, a team of wild gorillas armed with baseball bats would not persuade me to turn her down.

I was hooked on her attention and the smell of her, plus the fact that she was gorgeous. I wanted to steal her soul too; plus the rest of her, and some more at that. I needed to think, I was wallowing in a sea of confusion and physical indecision. She was having the effect of knocking all my caution to the winds and I feared I might frighten her with the truth of what I had just escaped from. She might run from me thinking I was a nut or something. I had to buy a little time. Diversionary tactics were called for.

'I think I need to eat,' I said. 'I will tell you when I fill this void that used to be my stomach.' I popped back into the bathroom with a change of clothing

and two minutes later we wandered down to the
buffet terrace just in time for a Nile sunset.
. Every night, the hotel put on classical music
through loudspeakers so those guests who so
desired could sit around the terrace to watch the
sunset before the evening meal was served. Tonight
the music was from La Boheme, my favourite
opera. We sat together and as the pathos of Rudolfo
and Mimi's meeting with a touch of hands 'che
gelida manina', 'your tiny hand is frozen', flowed
from the hi-fi.
I felt the tears come to my eyes as they always do
whenever I hear this passage of beautiful music. I
really tried not to show them, but Anna took my
hand in hers and said 'Simpatico Tu sai simpatico'.
Which is, as I understand, a great compliment in
Italian, as it means one has real feelings?

Chap 6

Every sunset over the Nile is different due to the
time of year, wind direction and variable cloud
patterns. This one was, to my still tired frame, the
portent of a rebirth. The iridescent landscape across
the river with the palm trees standing in black relief
against the deepening blue black sky and the last
golden highlights touching upon the peaks of the
desert hills beyond was enthralling and thought
provoking.

I could see the sky mirrored in the polished red
granite flagstones of the outdoor dance floor as we
sat together on the terraced seats facing west,
towards the Nile. I felt the water that had
condensed on my glass, trickle onto my leg. Anna
moved closer beside me making room as others
were joining the music. It was reassuring to be
amongst people who were not out to kill me for a
change.

I hoped that all the bad parts were now over, but
logic told me that was only a myth. As the myriad
colours reached like ethereal fingers across the
darkening heavens the flash of magic combined
with Puccini and her touch took me to a private
heaven. We were part of an eternal event and the
warm aroma of the evening flowers wafted spirit

like around us as though to tie with whispery traces
our souls to this moment in time.

Unfortunately all too soon, it was over and the
babble of conversations between guests took
precedent, destroying the muse.

I overheard the gossip, from an adjacent couple,
that two men had been killed in a gunfight over the
river and was it safe here with all the terrorists
around? I could not help but wince at the thought
of the escapade of the previous night, and thanked
my guardian angel for saving me for this
experience. I looked at Anna and silently prayed
that she too had found the previous hour of musical
sunset as fulfilling as I. The reflected lights from the
Nile now illuminated her face and the angle of
radiance enhanced her fine features with its glow.
Obviously she would not be too disturbed by the
idle comments that had broken the spell holding
me, for she had yet to know I had been the intended
victim or had been involved. She was not stupid
and it would not be long before Anna realised
exactly who the subject of the conversation was.
Would it change how she felt about me? I hoped
that it would not.

All of a sudden I felt the shock of the situation
coming like a dark heavy cloak over my shoulders.
It was too much to just try to laugh off by myself
and put down to just a stroke of bad luck. The

weight of responsibility was discernible now, as though it was increasing second by second. I realised that I must have been on autopilot for the last few hours. The fight or flight reflex had carried me until now but the adrenaline was running low.

I was more concerned how Anna thought of me than the unholy trouble I would be in if the authorities found out my involvement in a double; no make that a quadruple set of killings. Why this concern? I had only just met Anna. I could not explain the attraction I felt for her. It was strong and deep. It was not a sexual thing but a friendship beyond anything I had experienced before.

Of course I was attracted sexually but this cut through the normal getting to know you type of introductions. I felt that I should not try and analyse it too much, as it was very strangely enjoyable. Was I falling in love? Was it still only twenty-four hours ago? Should I throw the whole bloody lot into the Nile and forget all about it? Could I live with myself if I did? Should I involve this warm sympathetic lady in my sordid adventure? Does she feel the same way too about me?

The last question was answered in part when she turned to me and said 'It is a beautiful evening for lovers' that did it. I had to tell her. If we were to move on from this weird start, we would have no secrets.

I have always been a romantic but not a Romeo
and do firmly believe that people are smitten by
love. Why shouldn't Anna, be smitten by me? More
to the point what did she see in me? In reality I
think of myself as a cheerful individual with a
slightly elevated sense of humour, but not a
comedian. I am certainly not handsome but women
find me interesting, although throughout my life I
had had problems in the love race; I certainly was
not a winner but had been an also-ran on numerous
occasions. I felt now could be different with this
warm, attractive, and vivacious lady. Perhaps I
might just have found the right person for me.

We waited until the final notes had echoed and
come to rest. The evening was upon us, and the
lights from the boats making their way to Luxor
reflected like luminescent fish from the darkening
water. There was so much activity here, so many
people enjoying the place of legend that had
endured for thousands of years.

Getting up, I offered Anna my hand and she took it
in hers. Her touch was like a warm bath that
relaxed and engulfed me. The feeling washed over
my whole body and I momentarily basked in the
sheer pleasure of it. We walked slowly to the
restaurant. I felt like an adolescent again and was
glad of the darkness that hid my embarrassment at
this feeling.

The meal was sheer dream world, fantasy. The golden glow from the candle enhanced her flawless complexion and reflected like spiritual fire in her eyes. We talked and opened ourselves to each other as the bond of friendship grew silently, enveloping us both in a strange unreality. She was on vacation from her job as professor of astrophysics in Lyon, where she worked on the mapping of nebulae using photographic downlinks, from the Hubbell Space Telescope. I must confess she lost me at times but I was lost anyway.

She was forty and had been widowed five years previously by a tragic motor accident. Her husband and six-year-old son had plunged off an alpine road during a sudden downpour. She had concealed herself and her sorrows, in her work and this was her first excursion in an attempt to pick up her life. Three weeks ago Anna had buried the past and taken the first package holiday she found. I inwardly prayed that this was not going to be just a holiday romance. I hoped that fate had drawn us together and I secretly prayed that the future might be better for both of us.

Hurt and betrayal plus a lot of dishonesty and unfairness had painted my life a bitter shade of grey until this moment. I had been cynical and mistrusting of any woman who had got close enough to me; close enough that is for me to even contemplate loving her. That is not to say I am a misogynist but I was three parts of the way there. I had a normal sexual appetite and had enjoyed plenty of between the sheets loving but whenever marriage or commitment had been mentioned, I had retreated to my solitary parenthood. I had never involved my son Steven in my liaisons because I had not wanted him to get attached to a surrogate mother. My parents had filled that gap for him and had been a lifeline to my freedom. They had looked after Steve in my absence with love and affection; I really owed them for that.

I had never thought that I might love again, especially without questioning the background of the one I now believed in. I was falling, or had fallen in love with Anna.

I reflected on my life so far and realised that Anna was giving me uncompromising love. We just clicked. It was not a lust driven animal thing but a gentle cerebral merging, like two souls combining. Neither of us were spring chickens but it was not just looks and character that was driving us two together. She was beautiful, and I momentarily wondered what she saw in me. I realised that something powerful was really in charge of my emotions. I was experiencing a renaissance of consciousness and empathy.

If the rest of my life was going to be like this, then I wanted to live forever. As that thought made its passage through my head I had a feeling that perhaps I really had been living forever. I thought how stupid I'm getting; it must be the fright and excitement of the last twenty-four hours that is twisting my perception of reality. An old saying came to mind and I must have murmured it quietly 'The things we do by two and two; we pay for one by one' I looked at the radiant lady in front of me who was raising an eyebrow and gazing at me reflectively. I made up my mind that I was not going to perpetuate my life of solitude by upsetting her.

'Francis: you were miles away; look, you have not even touched your sweet' I was attracted by the candlelight that reflected from her eyes and replied stupidly 'I have no need of it as you are here' Anna laughed and I thought I saw the beginning of a tear. She took my hand and sweetly spoke 'that was so romantic. I was thinking that your eye must be sore' To tell the truth I had almost forgotten my aches and pains but my eye was a bit swollen, that plant had been sharp. 'You were lucky not to have lost your sight, Just stay like that for a few seconds, I want to show you something' So saying she took a small digital camera from her handbag; before I realised it she had taken a picture. 'Look at this

Francis' she turned the LCD screen towards me.
The Aloe Vera leaf had cut a shape like an inverted
V below my right eye. The shape made it look like
the Uchat or eye of Horus.
'That is strange, it certainly did not feel like that
when I did it.' The skin had puffed up a little and
the effect was certainly pronounced in the light of
the camera flash. Anna held my chin and gently
moved my head from side to side so that she might
better examine my eye. 'That is incredible! Your
eyelid is bruised so it looks as though you are
wearing mascara. That plus the cut and swelling,
have made you look like an Ancient Egyptian. I
wonder what it means?' I was unsure too and did
not know what to say, but a chill ran deep inside
my consciousness; I felt it would not be too long
before I found out.
'Now Anna, I will keep my word and explain the
events leading to our meeting. I first however must
get you to promise that what I shall tell you remain
a secret between us, and us alone. Your life and
mine might depend upon it.' She nodded her assent
and said sweetly 'I hope we shall have more than
one secret between us'. I laughed and so did she, at
the innuendo contained in the manner of her reply.
I continued 'You may feel this to be the chat up line
of the evening, but you will have to come to my
room to see what I am talking about'. I laughed at

my faux pas and we both dissolved into titters of childish laughter to the amusement of the other diners who smiled at our uninhibited happiness. We returned to my chalet, our path now illuminated by tiny fairy lights, through the smell of mimosa and eucalyptus, along the Nile bank past a gigantic game of chess. I felt as though it was unreal, the type of thing you see in the movies. We waltzed with pawns and kings and then each other to the sound of distant music, laughing all the way. We held each other as though we were long lost friends embracing like teenagers.

Why is it that moments like this only endure in truth for such a short time and remain in ones memory forever? We savoured this moment as though we both knew that it was a dream and had a sell by date.

My chalet lay ahead, the outside light on, welcoming us. We entered, still giggling.

The room had been devastated; everything was scattered around like the aftermath of an explosion. Broken items were strewn about as though a demon had rampaged through my case. I looked at the mini-bar, it had not been moved. Anna said sternly 'Yes Francis, you certainly owe me that explanation'. I just stood there numbed by the contrasting emotions I now felt. How the hell did they know it was me? How did they know where to find me? Who the hell were they? My life was becoming one great round of questions, which really needed answering. There was only one problem, I did not know the answers, and those who did, were not the types to give them in a nice manner, if their calling cards were anything to go by.

Chap 7

'Let's get out of here, ' I said with real conviction.
'Whoever did this may still be around and I do not
want to meet them.' I was convinced now that I had
been seen this morning; or even followed back to
the hotel.

Anna really looked stunned; her dream had been
shattered too. It really was painful for us both; we
had been enjoying ourselves. I had warned her that
things could be getting serious. That of course was
no conciliation.

I rushed over to the mini-bar and putting my hand
down behind it, I was relieved to find the knapsack
still there. I extricated my old shirt containing the
items I had bought throwing them down by the
bed, I took the knapsack and its contents that the
violators of my room had desired to find.

Shutting the door we both hurriedly retreated to
Anna's chalet where I pushed the knapsack, with its
contents, behind the mini-bar in her room, it had
served me once as a safe repository, and should do
so again.

While I was doing this, and before I could stop her,
Anna called reception, to report the damage to my
chalet. 'Hello, is that reception? Could you please
send security round to D3, there has been a
burglary. Yes, that is the one belonging to Mr.
Edwards.'

Realising I could not now cover things up I said,
'Anna, tell them I will meet them there'
I was getting a bit worried. This is the best way to
mess up a nice holiday. Not content with trying to
kill me, these people wanted to have another go at
my belongings.

Now I would have to waste half the night giving
statements to the inevitable policemen, and I really
could not give a good explanation as to why my
room should be trashed, or what it was they were
after.

I told Anna to lock her door, and then I returned
the short distance to my chalet to find that two
armed, uniformed security guards had already
arrived. I opened the door for them and they
roughly pushed me inside. A pistol was rammed up
my left nostril and a voice demanded to know the
whereabouts of the box.

It is amazing how the realisation of ones mortality
and the fear of its immediate implementation and
early arrival can galvanise and stimulate your
mind. In other words I was bloody scared.

I wanted the hell out of here. I was speechless with
apprehension. I could only stutter because my teeth
were chattering with fear. 'What box?' I said
pleadingly.

'Do you mean that?' I said indicating the shirt
containing the box I had bought that morning. It

was lying broken on the floor. 'I bought that last night from a man I met over the river' I looked at them as best I could 'I bought a bird too'

They looked at each other and one asked, 'Where is it?' I could smell the garlic of his last meal, and the rancid tobacco on his breath made me want to gag. 'Over there by the curtains' I said, using my eyes to indicate the general direction of my other morning's lucky purchase. 'Get it Abdul and hurry' the eldest said, pointing with the barrel of his weapon. Abdul moved over to the window, his feet scrunching on some broken article of mine

'Someone is coming so let's get out of here.' Said my captor, as Abdul bent to retrieve the useless item. I felt the hair on the back of my neck move as an arm came down with the butt of the pistol crashing painfully against my skull. I heard the crunch as it tore through my scalp. I felt a burning pain and coupled with a blinding flash I descended into darkness.

Again, I awoke to gaze into those lovely eyes. This time they were tormented by empathy and had obviously been weeping. I groaned at the pain that was holding a convention inside my head.

I felt bloody stupid, and smiled at the same time as the realisation of my situation again hit me. I seemed to be making a habit of this.

As my absent wits were returning on their river of pain, I became more aware of my surroundings. I was lying among my luggage, still in my room. There were others here too. Tourist police wearing black berets and their surplus British army uniforms and large badges on their arms denoting them as such were standing about like inquisitive statues.

A rather corpulent, extremely large man in an expensive suit, looking like a sumo wrestler, came over and started to give me the third degree. He had short cut hair and a slightly pointed head and wore a finely trimmed goatee beard and moustache, the type I would never have the patience to grow myself. Even if it had suited me.

' I am Khalid; I am Superintendent of Police why did these men want to rob you? Who were they? What did they want?' The strangeness of my present position seemed to be his main concern. Something, perhaps some premonition, told me that this man was no fool and that I had better be a bit careful what lies or story I told him. I proceeded to make it clear in no uncertain terms that it was I who should be asking those questions. I was only a tourist who had been in Egypt for three days, or was it four?

He seemed to relent and under pressure from the hotel manager who had been ruefully surveying the blitzkrieg of one of his precious chalets, Khalid allowed a doctor access to my bleeding aching head.

Anna held my hand and kept repeating words of endearment and consolation as she explained that not wishing to stay alone in her room and being worried that I might get hurt, she had followed me at a distance and had seen my abduction by the two phoney policemen.

She had then run to intercept the genuine security personnel and had hurried them into action.

The local police had already been called when she had phoned reception and had arrived in force within minutes much to the chagrin of the management and the entertainment of the guests. There had been a hurried manhunt in the vicinity of my chalet and a couple of suspicious individuals had been discovered by an elderly guest trying to get into her bedroom. Her subsequent wails had called up the posse.

They were now in pursuit of the two intruders, who had run off and escaped in a waiting boat, which had been moored to the jetty not a hundred metres from my chalet.

Anna went on to tell me that there had been lots of shouting and gunshots on the river about five minutes before I awoke.

 More than that she did not know. My head was throbbing like a demented road drill and my ears were ringing enough to outdo Quasimodo.

Someone suggested that I be removed for better medical attention and I allowed myself to be assisted to Anna's chalet; just a short stumble down the fragrant path.

On entering, I simply fell into the room as my balance finally failed me completely. I collapsed on the first bed I saw and the room continued to spin and rock. Like surfing a tsunami in a hurricane.

 The doctor said something and inserted a needle into a phial of something. I felt a jab in my arm, and the world was plunged again into darkness. As I slipped down into this enveloping, soothing state, I could feel her hand tighten onto mine long after my pain and consciousness had gone.

Chap 8

It was still dark when I returned to consciousness.
Anna was still beside me, only I was lying tucked
up in bed. She sat, fast asleep, fully clothed,
propped up against the headboard. The bathroom
light was on and the door cast its shadow over the
bed. In the available light, I could see we were in
her room. I felt something wrapped around my
head. I gently lifted my hand to investigate, and
was dismayed when she stirred and shook herself
awake. She groaned a little as the obviously
uncomfortable position had cramped her neck. As
attentive as always she stroked my arm and
reached over me to hand me a drink. I felt that I
could really love this woman. I turned to her and
saw the box with the painting on the lid lying on
the bed.

Our eyes met and she said 'Forgive me Francis;
please do not be angry with me. I had to know why;
you were robbed and beaten. While you were
asleep, I took the liberty of examining this
wonderful thing. I think I might have an answer for
you. Before I do however, how do you feel? '

I could only croak a plaintive reply. Whilst assured
I had meant the affirmative, she explained ' the
doctor has put four stitches in your head and
suspects you may be concussed for a few days. He

also told you to rest and keep still but I am sure you have no intention of obeying.'

I drank deeply. I certainly needed fluid. That gerbil in my head was angry again and was making my eyes water. 'Would you have a Paracetamol?' I asked. I staggered to my feet and made my way to the bathroom. I felt queasy and certainly needed the loo. Understandingly, Anna let me go, respecting my sense of pride. 'Don't lock the door. I do not want to call anyone if you pass out again. We need some peace.'

I returned, having splashed copious quantities of water over my face and also having brushed my teeth. Anna had even brought my toothbrush from among the debris of my wrecked room. What a lady!

I was less annoyed by my circumstances because of her genuine kindness and care. 'Let's get down to it then. What have you found Anna?' Not giving her time to reply, I leant over her and kissed her gently, full on the lips.

She relaxed and hugged me close so that I overbalanced and fell onto her. I slipped onto the floor and started giggling all over again. 'You are mad,' she said, turning on her side to pull me up again.

I got to my feet and sat down beside her. She slid to the other side of the bed and took the box in her hands putting it on the bedside table.

With a sensual glint in her eye she looked me up and down saying 'Now or later?' 'Not tonight, I have a headache' I said still laughing. We both dissolved into fits of laughter for at least five minutes. Neither of us could look at the other without giggling.

Whether it was the stress or the events I had both witnessed, and been involved in, I will never know but that laughter brought such relief and peace to me. The presence of Anna, was augmented by joy and happiness contrasted against the horrors of last night. I was fully aware again, of my own mortality and the fact that I now had someone to live for.

'Please tell me what you have found,' I said.

Anna turned on the bedside light; taking the box she placed it between us. She took a magnifying glass and proceeded to explain.

' When we brought you back here it was because I did not want them to take you to hospital Francis. I put you to bed and sat wondering what was going on, Since you had promised to tell me about it and I had made my promise to you; I felt you would not mind if I looked in the bundle you had hidden in my room.'

I nodded my assent and promptly regretted the movement of my head. Making a mental note to keep it still I put her mind at ease and asked her to continue.

'I do not know how you got this box. I have not yet opened it, as I wanted to get a scientific evaluation of it, and its contents. I thus examined the picture. Not being conversant with Egyptology I did not see its significance. '

' It is the judgement of Thoth; the weighing of the soul of the dead.' I interjected.

'That may be so Francis. The point I am making is that I was not looking at the picture just for its sake, I was looking at everything, and being conversant with the stars and constellations, I was more interested in those shown in the picture.

Look at this one here. It is Orion. This one is Ursa Major or you might call it the Big Dipper.' Her finger pointed to the little marks on the box. They were tiny.

'Anna how do you know that? ' I asked. Without reply she put the lens in my hand, and with her face pressed close so she could focus it for me, brought the tiny marks into the shape of the constellation of The great bear.

Well it was stretched a bit and looked on its side but with a small amount of imagination, and the knowledge that I was in the presence of a doctor of

Astronomy I was convinced. Nevertheless, I was amazed and listened intently as she continued.

'To be quite truthful, I thought this was a forgery because the view of that constellation is from more northerly latitude.

I then thought that with the wobble of the earth, on its axis relative to space; that this could have been how the stars looked about four to five thousand years ago.

I would have to run a computer program to find out, but it is possible, yes, very possible.'

Her already wonderful eyes sparkled even more brightly with her inner knowledge as she continued.

'You will notice that there are a lot of stars shown as crosses just like a plus sign. These are the minor stars. The more bright stars are shown as having eight points or a cross with an x superimposed.

I shall have to explain a little basic astronomy to convince you of the date of this box. If you live in the Northern Hemisphere the most important star in the night sky is Polaris; people usually call by its more descriptive name of 'North Star'.

Actually, both names describe it well. The Earth's spin is such that the axis of our rotation points to Polaris, so Polaris appears over the North Pole. That's why it's called the 'North Star'. Everyone in the ancient world was able to find Polaris, assuming, clouds did not cover it.

 The best way to find it is to use some of the brightest stars that point to it. So the first thing to identify is the Big Dipper. Some people, mistakenly, call the Big Dipper a constellation.

 The Big Dipper is only a part of a bigger constellation called Ursa Major, the Big Bear, but the Dipper is obvious. The two stars furthest from the handle point to Polaris. They are often nicknamed 'the Pointers but their correct names are Merak and Dubhe. If you imagine a line from Merak through Dubhe and beyond, you will soon arrive at a star of similar brightness, which is the North Star.'

 Anna was now making sense. I was enthralled as she continued. 'This view of the northern sky seems to be from long ago, so I began to think about those times, all those years ago, and to try to understand the people who made this picture.

 What was the purpose of showing specific constellations? What is the purpose of this box?

 I feel that the picture is concealing the reason. Not being knowledgeable enough, I am a bit confused. There is a way to get a specific time and date from the aspect of these stars, but to do so would require the use of a sophisticated computer program, or a lot of luck.

Does it tell us anything? I believe it is trying to. Can you shed some light on the matter Caro?'

The closeness of her almost caused me to break my earlier resolution not to move, as her warm breath on my neck moved my libido up a notch. She had just called me dear.

I used the magnifying glass to examine the catch and hinges. I noticed a number of baboons painted around the edge of the box. I knew that the ancient Egyptians took baboons to be the guardians of the hours because they seemed to welcome the rising sun every morning.

I also noticed a disk with an Uchat eye set in its centre. There were four dots around it. That was strange, I recognised it immediately. It was so obvious but why was it shown here?

'My God. Anna you were right. Doesn't Jupiter have four moons and a big red spot?' I handed her the box and excitedly pointed to that portion I had been examining. By not taking the scene for granted we had opened up what might be the true meaning of its story.

Anna looked at my discovery and the realisation hit us both simultaneously. Without even a lens, all that we saw represented here could not be seen by the naked eye. Without the use of a telescope Jupiter was just a white dot in the heavens.

It needed a pretty good telescope to see the four moons Io, Ganymede, Callisto and Europa. Who in ancient Egypt could have drawn this, three and a half thousand years before the invention of the telescope?

Chap 9

It was several minutes before the shock of
realisation left us. Why would people be prepared
to rob and kill for this object? It was more of a
conundrum than a relic.

To my knowledge alone, four persons were dead
because of this box and its contents. Also
considering that was only in the last two days and
only the number I actually knew about. It was
obvious that even knowing about its existence was
perilous and possibly fatal. So I decided to tell Anna
immediately.

Putting the box down, I held her close so that her
head was resting on my shoulder. I recounted the
previous nights adventure and took her back the
short number of hours before I had joined the bus.
Leaving out nothing I revealed the experiences and
horrors of the previous night, and when I had
finished the early morning sun was reaching into
the room with a gentleness that marked a new day.
She had lain silent, only moving slightly when I
described the suicide of the villain.

I too shuddered when I recalled the horror and fear
I had felt lying up on the temple pylon at Medinet
Habu.

I got up and went to the mini-bar. I was still a bit
shaken but now adrenaline and excitement took

over. I wanted a cold drink, as my throat was dry.
Asking Anna if she desired one also, I recalled the
documents I had also taken. Would they give a clue
to these events?

'I'll have a coke please. ' She said drowsily. So,
having poured two glasses, I brought them along
with the rest of my spoils still in my knapsack, back
to the bed.

She lay there, illuminated by the dawn that had
percolated the curtains, and I could see the tiny
hairs on her sunburnt arms, as the obliqueness of
the morning sunlight caught her in its luxuriant
golden glow.

The moment gone, she sat up, taking the chilled
glass from me; she sipped the contents with delight.
I suddenly found that I enjoyed just simply
watching her.

She was elegant and refined but ever so human and
fragile. I remembered the tears in those eyes, they
had been for me, and I was grateful for them.

'Let's have a look through these papers. They may
tell us something. Anna, would you read this bunch
please? I shall read the rest after I have had a look
at these two boxes. I don't know what we are
looking for, I hope we can make some sense of the
whole lot.'

Anna took the few papers from me and I noticed
how tired she looked. 'Do you feel up to it or would

you like to get some sleep?' I said with real concern.
'We are going to have to rest soon'. She replied 'I
would like to at least find out the names of those
men you told me about, and where they came from.
Please hand me the passports.'
' I think we should be careful not to leave any
fingerprints on them Anna. Eventually we will have
to do something about this. We cannot keep it a
secret much longer as the police know I am
involved in something or other. '
 Anna got up and rummaged around her wardrobe
and produced a couple of thin polythene bags.
Putting them on her hands she took the documents
and held them beneath the bedside lamp. Opening
them she exclaimed.
'Look here they are both Egyptian names. The
passports are American. That is strange. Francis,
You did not mention they were Arabs.' 'I had no
idea, they spoke with American accents, at least that
is what I thought I heard. Do you think it is
significant?' She thought for a moment and replied.
'It may well be that these are false. Can you identify
the portraits?' Anna held the passport so that I
could see the page.
 I looked at the miniature pictures, and taking the
magnifying glass, I looked again. I couldn't be sure
but I felt that the one I was now examining was of
the unfortunate, who had blown his brains out not

fifty feet from me. His name had been Kemal Abdul Nagir. He had been twenty-six only three days ago. As old as Steven; what a waste I thought.

 Anna opened the second passport and held it under the lamp. The other photograph showed a smiling man who had a small moustache; he was called something Aziz. I could not read his forename as it had been obliterated by his own blood, he had been twenty-four.

 I could not feel any empathy for those two; they had clearly been out to kill me. Nevertheless, some mother or woman would grieve, when they did not return.

I said. 'I can see nothing here, other than names, and I do not know them either. Can I have one of those bags please? I would like to look through these' Anna removed one and gently put it on my hand.

 I took the passports and flicked the pages open with the handle of the magnifying glass. 'There are entry visas though, they are from Heliopolis and these guys entered Egypt ten days ago. Obviously they were in Cairo before coming to Luxor, but why?'

Meanwhile Anna was examining some of the papers I had also retrieved from the case along with the money. Suddenly she sat bolt upright, which, compared to her obvious tiredness of a few minutes before, scared the hell out of me.

'What is it?' I said shakily 'That's it. They are looking for somewhere, but they need something to lead them to wherever it is they seek!' She pointed to a paragraph. I put the passports on the bedside table and moved closer to her

Anna passed me the piece of paper she had been studying and let me read it. The print was smudged but it had been generated on some typewriter or other. It was a tiny bit indistinct, but the meaning was obvious to me. There was evidence, it said of certain artefacts from the tomb of Hatshepsut having come onto the market. One such item was a statue of a falcon. This item had been reported found near Luxor.

Using the magnifying glass I examined it more closely. It had been typed on an old fashioned machine which had misaligned the letter n. The letter went on to instruct the persons to offer cash to the value of two hundred thousand dollars just to borrow it. There were also instructions on keeping in touch and some numbers, which I took to be either co-ordinates or telephone numbers.

'Can you believe it?' I exclaimed. 'Those two intended to double-cross whoever engaged them to find these bits and pieces. They only wanted to borrow them too.' Anna looked incredulously at me and I at her. What secret did these items hold? The mystery surrounding them was deepening by the hour.

I examined the two thin metal boxes. That had been hidden in the briefcase One was a very modern Global Positioning System. The other was a strange folding, slim line; Mobile Telephone that attached to a minute dish that unfolded from the box.

A green light centred in a dish symbol seemed to indicate if communication was possible. A simple on off slide switch completed the package. This was a state of the art spy set-up. It was something out of Mission Impossible.

I was unable to comprehend this. Who was after the box? Who would have access to this type of equipment? Why had I been attacked? It didn't make sense.

Anna said 'Let's hide this and get some sleep. I am absolutely tired, stanco morto as we say in Italy.'

I nodded agreement and proceeded to separate the items.

The passports I would wipe off and deposit in the Nile. It was only fair that they be identified. It was the only way I could think of without giving myself away.

The papers could be secreted in any of the pamphlets or guidebooks on the table.

The electronics could be put behind the water tank
in the bathroom. The treasures as yet unseen by us
would be put outside, away from interference. The
former was easy.

I got up and prepared the passports, cleaning away
any evidence of contact with Anna or myself.
I put the boxes out of sight and returned to the
bedroom. Anna lay fast asleep, her bosom rising
and falling rhythmically. I blew her a kiss and
placed the papers as planned.

With the passports wrapped in a piece of carrier
bag, which I had wiped also I left the room closing
the door gently, after having made sure I had the
Key. It would not do to lock myself out and disturb
her unnecessarily.

A fluttering sound behind me made me jump. It
was only a sparrow. I would have to be careful as I
was becoming a bit paranoid.

Keeping the chalet in sight, not wanting to leave her
I made my way to the riverbank.

The eucalyptus trees now irradiated by the low
morning sunshine cast their shadows over the path.
I could smell the oil in the leaves as I brushed
against their hanging branches. It was soothing and
strange at the same time.

Stepping into the shade, I carefully watched all
points of access for at least five minutes before I
trusted that I was not being observed or followed.

I never let my eyes be distracted for more than seconds at a time from the chalet door. I now stood on the bank of the Nile and could see both up and downstream.

There was a cruise ship about a hundred metres to my left. I could see the stern with the navigation lights still visible. It was making its way towards its final destination at Aswan. I also saw a small rowboat with a man casting his net on the other side of the river.

A felucca was also there with its sail set to catch the breeze that blew in the early morning as it too proceeded upriver. It was tacking away from me. It was now or never. I eased the plastic wrapped package from my pocket making sure I left no fingerprints, and dropped it on the ground. Glancing around again I checked the chalet. Still deserted.

I booted the package as hard as possible. It sailed in a gentle arc, over the papyrus fronds that clustered around the bank and landed with a discernible splash disturbing an Ibis that had been waiting for breakfast.

The package floated as I had hoped and I watched it get caught in the current as it meandered along with a clump of lotus plants. Hopefully, it would be found downstream.

Still suspicious of everything, I looked around for a
safe place in which to secrete the treasure.

 My eyes were drawn to the large chess set we had
played with the previous evening. I reached out
and picked up a piece. It was relatively heavy and
was made of painted wood, with the various
sections screwed into one another.

 I started examining its construction. There was a
void in the body of the pawn I had chosen. I took
the white king into the shade and unscrewed the
crown. There was a void here as well, but larger.

 I checked for size and was delighted to find that
the box would just fit into the cylindrical cavity,
which was about 15 centimetres in diameter and
just as deep.

 I glanced towards the chalet; someone was coming.
I emptied the contents from the box and put it
inside the chess-piece. I quickly screwed the crown
back on, tightening it more than before.

 It would not do if anyone else was to open it, but I
would have to take the risk. I replaced it in position
on the chequered surface.

 Now bending low as not to be seen and crouching
down, behind the hedge I retreated beyond the
chessboard and stood up behind a eucalyptus tree.
Pretending to be idly watching the Nile, I waited as
the person, a maid or something, passed by the
games area. The hiding place would have to do.

At least one item was relatively safe. I returned to the chalet, quietly letting myself in as not to wake my sleeping beauty. I too lay on the bed and was soon fast asleep.

Chap 10

I sat up in panic, and looked around the room. My head was being subjected to a stampede of gerbils this time round. My headache was equivalent to all the world cup teams having used it as a football, and kicked it into touch. It was almost blinding; I found things difficult to bring into focus. It was obviously afternoon because the sunrays were from the other side of the window now. That I could tell. I felt for the bottle of Paracetamol and took a few, chewing them for maximum speed. Their bitter taste brought on a thirst like the Sahara. I made my way to the bathroom, using the wall and anything I could lean onto as a guide. I groped around and found the light-switch, turned it on, and looked into the mirror. A man wearing a bloodstained turban gazed back at me, through eyes that were filled with blood. God, I looked absolutely awful as usual. It was difficult to look at anything for long. It was difficult to see at all. The room seemed to close in on me and I swayed, and ended up leaning over the sink. I turned on the cold tap and with cupped hands, poured a stream of not quite cold water over my head and into my mouth. The bandage came off, and the subsequent cooling of my skull was a relief. Obviously, since I had been cooking my brain, this was having the desired effect. I staggered into the shower and enjoyed a more forceful cold dunking, whilst using the faucet as a handrail. I have no idea how long it took, but things were not spinning so much. Turning off the cooling stream I splashed out of the shower, water cascading onto the floor. I removed my clothes and was surprised when my shirt caught on the stitches that spread over the back of my head. I dried myself, which was not too difficult because of the heat and on looking at the mirror again I was encouraged to see a message in lipstick which said 'Out to lunch'. That pleased me, because it meant that at least, Anna was all right and I had not been having a nightmare.

I sat on the loo, holding my poor head and gradually brought my tortured mind up to date. I found conscious thought painful, so I just let my memory return at a pace less traumatic for me. I felt that if I were to spruce myself up a little, I would feel better.

This time I shaved more carefully and did not make the usual surgical modifications to my face. I changed into the last set of undamaged clothing I possessed. Finding some bandages, I bound up my head untidily; I did not want to catch my stitches unnecessarily. The headache was now abating like the aftermath of a thunderstorm. I could feel it rolling away with every beat of the throbbing rhythm, becoming less strident, .as the analgesic effects of the chewed tablets cut in.

Fresh air was what I needed now I thought. I put on my sunglasses, and was just about to open the door when I heard low voices outside. Looking around the edge of the long curtain that was shading the room I was able to observe the pathway to my door, without being seen. Outside, I saw the portly form of the policeman Khalid, whom I had seen the night before. He was talking to what I took to be a real security guard and, was pointing at the door as if asking him to open it.

I replaced the curtain, being careful not to make it obvious, and grabbing the Ivory box and the statue off the bedside table; I put them in the toilet cistern, knowing that water would not hurt them. Then I heard the key in the door. Quickly I pulled my tee shirt half over my head taking care not to disturb my stitches and sat down on the bed.

Pretending to be putting it on, I rose in feigned indignation that this man had entered both without knocking and without my permission. 'What the hell are you doing here?' I shouted, hoping I could set the tone as being indignant and putting him at an immediate disadvantage as I had the last time we met. I then launched, into a tirade of protest. 'I am a poor tourist who has been burgled and beaten up, robbed and injured, open your eyes and just

look at me, so what are you and your police force
doing to catch the crooks?' I let out a few expletives
as I described the treatment and added 'I shall be
reporting this to my tour company and to your
ministry of tourism'.

All this seemed to hit him, Khalid pondered for a
moment and offering me the palms of his hands in
supplication he started to withdraw, apologising
profusely and bowing like a Humpty Dumpty toy.

 I was feeling a bit sorry for him as he had an
important job to do and I was just being obstinate
and unhelpful.

 I smiled and said disarmingly, 'Please, If you wish
to see me, or enter my room. No, this is not my
room. All the same I would demand the respect of a
knock at the door and my presence here when you
call. I do feel it is wrong for you to enter a guest's
bedroom without permission, or their knowledge.
Any way, what could you hope to find?'

He gyrated his massive form and spoke ' I am truly
sorry Mr Edwards. I meant no harm. You were not
exactly capable of giving me a reasonable
explanation last night.

 This afternoon, two passports were found at
Karnak, which as you know is about seven
Kilometres downriver from here.'

'What has that to do with me?' I asked him.
Looking straight into his eyes as innocently as I
possibly could. He gazed back and said
' I am not sure. But perhaps they belonged to the
two men who attacked you last night?' I am not a
Sherlock Holmes, but I could see he was trying to
trap me.
If the protection I had given them had been
effective, and it obviously had. The passports had
stayed afloat, and had been found. It would have
been obvious to him that the owners were already
dead, and in police custody, in some morgue or
other.
 He knew that they matched the two dead men over
the river. He wanted me to deny it without seeing
them first, thus proving my involvement. For how
could I know, without looking at the photographs
within them, if they belonged to my most recent
attackers?
'Come on Khalid, I said, do you think I am psychic?
Let me see if I can identify them.' It seemed to
work.
He fished in his pocket and withdrew the passports
I had taken so much care to dispose of that
morning. Each was inside a polythene bag and open
so that the photographs were visible without
having to touch them. Handing them to me, he was
watching my face intently.

I felt that I should give as little away as I possibly could, so with a serious look I turned them as though it was the first time I had seen them.
'Hey, these are American passports. The men who attacked me certainly were not Americans.' I added seeming confused. 'Most probably, some tourist has dropped these.' I added as ignorantly as I could, 'It looks as though they have got wet' and examining the one with blood on it, I dropped it in mock horror; 'Ugh! This one has got blood on it!' He seemed convinced, but I was not too sure. I would have to watch him very carefully.
 He suspected, quite rightly, that I knew more than I was telling. I had better be on my guard at all times. I wanted him on my side but could I trust him? It would be prudent to wait until Anna and I knew who was involved
Khalid and I nearly cracked heads as we both instinctively bent down to retrieve the fallen passport. That would not have done me any good at all as my headache had almost disappeared. I thought that he seemed very agile for a man of his size. I looked at the photograph closely, and then I handed the passport back to him, saying was sorry, both for dropping it and that I did not know that person, which of course was true.
I examined the other for a while longer, making sure that if I had left prints on it previously, I would

confuse the issue now by squeezing the bag and
rubbing it against any possible print I might have
left there.

Neither document had suffered too much from its
Nile cruise. 'No' I said, pausing for effect 'I honestly
do not know this one either, but he does seem
slightly familiar. He looks like someone who was
on the plane or at the airport.' This seemed to
satisfy Khalid. He smiled, thanked me for trying
and expressed his profuse sorrow at having
interrupted me.

'Did you catch those burglars last night? My friend
says that there were gunshots soon after I was
knocked out. We have not been told anything.' 'I
am so sorry Mr Edwards, perhaps I should confide
in you.' He said smilingly. 'Yes we managed to
shoot one of them, but the other one you know as
just Abdul could not be found. The dead man was
known to be a dishonest person, but until last night
we did not realise he was violent too.' He now
looked me straight in the eyes; I could see his
expression change slightly as he realised the extent
of my injuries.

'You see now Mr Edwards, why I ask these
questions. What do you have that would make men
kill for?' I held his gaze and just shrugged my
shoulders, turning my palms up. I thought I had
better not overdo it too much. 'I really have no idea

Superintendent but if I think of anything, I will let
you know.' Giving me a beautifully scripted
business card and begging me to get in touch,
should I recall anything, no matter how
insignificant it might appear to me; he left.

Chap 11

I stood, watching this enigmatic man walk away
and felt that I should consider my position. I was
now suspected of involvement and it would not be
too difficult for the police to find out my
movements yesterday and the day before. All it
would take would be a word from one of my co-
tourists from the coach yesterday to put me in the
area alone. Perhaps he had already found that out?
A few seconds later, Anna came along the path. She
wore a yellow summer dress with a halter-top,
which accentuated her figure. There was a spring in
her step, borne of having rested and eaten. The low
hedges only allowed me to see the top half of her
lithe, sun-tanned body. Seeing me standing in the
shade of the doorway, she waved and the look of
joy and happiness that lit up her pretty face, was
every-mans dream. Quickening her pace, she flew
to me as though she had hidden wings.
Her arms enveloped me and I felt the warmth of her
body pressing me backward into the room. Her lips
were like cherries, soft and succulent. I feasted I
really fell in Love. Kicking the door shut and
making sure we would not be disturbed, she said,
Looking at my turban style bandages; 'Well my red
eyed desert prince, take me away from all this'
We made love as though it had been invented just
for us. Our hunger for each other was enchanting

and fulfilling. The years and the pain rolled back for us both. We were young again. When, much later, we had descended back to the realness of the situation still holding and hugging, each other; we just languished in the feelings we stirred within each other.

The lateness of the hour enhanced by my stomach, complaining at not having been filled broke the mood so I let Anna know of my intention to get some new clothes and something to eat. 'We will have to go into town.' I said. 'I will get a taxi. I'm starving and could do with a beer too.' She gazed at me and said jokingly ' you men are all the same. Romance and beer.'

'I prefer the romance, ' I said, tickling her in a very strategic place. 'There are few things that would take me away from such beauty and pleasure, but thirst is certainly one of them.' We showered and fooled around a lot more. I did not really want to go out at all but room service would not stretch to new clothes.

The hour was getting late; we left the chalet with the statue and box, which we hid, behind the towel bin beside the pool. I easily slipped it between the restraining brick wall and the hedge; it would be safe until we returned. It seemed that chalet rooms were too easy to search and that no one would suspect this public place. We would have to return

past the pool when we had finished our business in
Luxor. I had put on one of her tee shirts, and looked
the part of a tourist. I would not escape close
scrutiny but it made us both laugh, as the bandage
on my head was partially hidden under a baseball
cap. I must have looked like an overgrown
schoolboy.

After bartering with the taxi driver regarding the
cost of the trip, we entered a mobile mosque, which
served as his taxi. There were curtains on the
windscreen and prayers in Arabic festooned around
like the banners of Mardi gras. The most
incongruous item was a Manchester United
supporter's scarf, which acted as a sun visor.
The driver, when he realised I was just a mad
English tourist kept on asking me if I knew Eric
Cantonna, David Beckham or the entire Manchester
and Leeds united teams. I found it moving and
humbling that one so hard working and
underprivileged would set as his heroes, the
overpaid, overindulgent British football
establishment. His knowledge of English football
folklore was just amazing and entertained us both.
We were surprised at his enthusiasm, especially
here, where football pitches were as rare as rocking
horse droppings.

We made our way to Luxor and were deposited by
the beginning of the main market area beside the

magnificent temple with its giant lotus and papyrus columns that forms the centre of the one-way system. The late afternoon sun bathed and enhanced the redness of the stone as it slid down towards the pyramidal mountain that lay at the head of the Valley of the Kings across the river to the west.

Looking down the Corniche de Nile I counted no less than six Nile cruise ships moored together. They were side by side as though lined up for a race. Owing to the small number of moorings, and the proliferation of gigantic cruise ships. All the ships tie up alongside each other, aligning their entrances, which conform to a standard height. So if your ship is last to dock, you have to make your way through the reception areas of many floating hotels, before you are able to go ashore. It is a veritable pontoon bridge that can stretch halfway across the river.

We walked along, hand in hand away from the river towards the shops. The tooting sounds of the numerous taxis, and the clip clop of the gaily decorated, horse drawn carriages, which drew up beside us, assailed our ears. 'Caleesh Caleesh, where to sir and madam? Very good prices.' would be the order of greeting. I told Anna not to catch their eyes, as this would be taken as a maybe. Anna being of a kind disposition seemed to strike up a

conversation with them all, much to my annoyance
as I was hungry and was myself being accosted by
every shopkeeper between here and Timbuktu.
Come on I said. Please be quick, as I am hungry.
'I like that fire in your eyes when you are angry, or
is it just the reflection of the sun?' She replied and
laughed; I could not sustain my annoyance in the
presence of this woman. I did however turn to the
assembled touts and Caleesh drivers and shout
cheekily 'maffi fluis imshi' which loosely translated
means bugger off I'm broke. Amid well-meaning
laughter and good wishes, we were left alone. I
really liked these people. Anna gazed at me
quizzically and asked innocently 'Was it something
I said?' 'No' I replied. 'It was something I said.' I
told her and she looked quite shocked, then she just
burst into those giggles I was beginning to fall in
love with. 'Let's eat,' She said, tugging me towards
a reasonably respectable restaurant which had a
sign that said Amun; many European tourists were
sitting at the pavement tables.' This looks safe
enough. So no gippy tummy'
We sat down, ordered a something to eat and
enjoyed watching the world go by. The diversity of
colours, animals, people, and the noise made an
interesting backdrop to a delicious meal. A sodium
lamp fixed to the mosque wall opposite me across
the square came on and within minutes went off; it

continued thus throughout the meal and was at times quite distracting. The call to final prayer, Allah u Akbar, la Illaha Illal Allah. God is great, I confirm there is no other God, stuttered from the loudspeakers hung from a minaret and shortly groups of worshipers arrived and entered the holy building.

Anna and I were like two halves of a single entity. We shared the experience and enjoyed the little nuances of the changing kaleidoscope of humanity that passed by. It was just sufficient for us to look in each other's eyes to share a laugh or pass unspoken comment on what we were observing.

This was fantastic. I had never shared such empathy with another person, as I did now. I seemed to know what Anna liked, and she knew what I liked. The amazing thing was that they were not always the same. It was uncanny how two lost souls could find each other so compatible, so soon. I began to hope that this would go on forever, and was just about to ask Anna if she felt the same, when her eyes opened wide and she indicated something behind me.

A voice said. 'Mr Edwards? I would like you to come with me'

Chap 12

'Please hurry Mr Edwards. There is not much time'. I turned to see a scruffy man in a faded brown galabia. He wore a crocheted skullcap or Topi in the Moslem style. I say scruffy because it looked as if he had been pulled through the dust. This was odd to me since I knew that, by his wearing the cap, he had obviously been to pray. He should have been clean, having carried out the ritual ablutions of his religion before prayer. This made me suspicious and I hesitated.

'Please Mr Edwards please come. My friend cannot wait, you must see him.' Turning to Anna who was trying to understand the situation, he said 'Madam, Jibril said, you may come too' ' Why did you not mention that name sooner?' I asked him. 'I am sorry sir, but I am to bring you as fast as a hawk. That is what Jibril said.' I then understood the cryptic message to be truly from my friend. 'Why did he send you?' I asked him, but he was by now, turning to leave. 'Sir you must hurry.' He said, looking around suspiciously. He began to leave our table so I called to him 'Please wait a moment I must pay first. I do not want to be arrested.' I beckoned the waiter over and asked him how much I owed. He quickly calculated and told me. Thrusting enough money at him I made our apologies for the abrupt departure. I too looked around to see why this fellow had rushed off so quickly, I saw nothing to alarm me so I took hold of Anna's hand, and hurried off to try and catch up with our emissary who was being swallowed up in the evening melee. He had definitely come from Jibril, so I did not want to lose him.

As we were racing along surrounded in mayhem, dust, filth and noise, I shouted an apology to Anna for my rough handling of her. She gave me a grin and replied. 'What an adventure, it beats watching television. We never seem to have a dull moment.' I would not say we have had a day of peace since we met'. Anna was fit, more agile than I was, she would whip in and out of traffic and people like a cruise missile. I gave up worrying about her safety and concentrated more on my own.

We left the brightly lit area and were soon off the main thoroughfare into the darker side streets. Never once did our guide turn to see if we were still behind him. I did notice that we were travelling parallel to the Nile as I could see the river cruisers moored on my left down some of the side streets we passed. I also tried to note some of the street signs like the Luxor Museum, just in case we had to find our way back in a hurry. His scurrying form was very difficult to keep track of because we were being hassled by all and sundry. I found myself getting a bit short of breath and my headache was threatening to return. Why would Jibril want us to come so quickly? Could he not have chosen a better place for a meeting?

The answer astounded both of us, for we were led into a courtyard and by the ambulances parked outside I took it to be a hospital. We followed at a more respectable pace now, to a blue-grey door that the man now held open for us to enter. As we passed him he panted out 'Hurry Mr Edwards, Madam'.

There was a wooden wall facing us with a grimy glass window set into its top. The patina of age had coloured it to a soft dark colour. There were posters on it, glued, taped and stapled. All of them informing the poor patients of some health measure in Arabic. He led us to a door on my left and opened it. Inside, as still as death lay my friend Jibril. He was clothed in white and without bed covers, lying on a metal-framed bed. It looked to me that he was waiting for fate to find him. He turned his face towards us as our guide withdrew, shutting the door behind him. He smiled, and spoke in his gentle voice to Anna and then pointing towards me 'I see you have a sense of adventure. You are getting involved with this good man' I was embarrassed and shocked at his condition. Not two days ago I had feared him. He looked so shrunk now, and far older than that evening. I tried not to convey my feelings in my expression as I came close to him. I said, 'Jibril, my friend, what has happened? Why are you here?

' 'Do not be alarmed Francis. I was not harmed the other night. The bad men came. I told them what we agreed, that I had sold the things a while ago. I then had a heart attack. My wife started wailing and woke up half the village. They left quickly enough then. Did I give you enough time Francis?

'Yes Jibril, I heard the noise and feared the worst for you and your family' I then proceeded to tell him the full story of my escape on top of the temple, my meeting Anna and my subsequent attack by two more men. Jibril smiled and told me to watch out for Khalid 'He is a very honest and clever man Francis. He is very powerful too. I do not dislike him but he has his own ways of justice'

I looked around the room and was upset that my friend was languishing here in such poor surroundings. Anna sat down on the only other piece of furniture in the room, a small table, and asked Jibril if there was anything he wanted. 'Yes, I would like to die in my own bed. Not today though, perhaps when the time is right.'

I said ' Jibril do you need special medical treatment or medicine or anything at all?' Jibril was adamant that there was nothing that needed doing at present and that he was grateful for our concern. I felt really guilty. He had given me a priceless object and was in a pauper's bed.

'When we met Francis, I was sure that you could help. There is an empathy within us all and you have it.' Jibril turned to Anna who was nodding assent. ' I can see that this pretty lady agrees with me. You are at present thinking how to do something for me because of the items I gave you. You are wrong to feel guilty because it is you who have been robbed and assaulted, you took the problems from me and onto yourself; and all because you trusted an old man who you had just met. You see that there is more than value to things. There is spiritual value to be gained from something so ancient. It was not in your mind or nature, to take these things to sell for profit. You see Francis; there was something more than the items I gave you. There was a legend of as scroll that told of a man such as yourself who would learn the way.'

Certainly Jibril had an air of mystery about him once inside his outward seemingly intimidating exterior; more due to him looking like some mad warlock, there was a sensitive caring person. I knew he had risked his life to give me the boxes but I could not understand why he had chosen me.

I was a tiny bit embarrassed again, but happy that I had been accepted by fate to perform whatever it was I had to do. Jibril continued. 'When one goes through life it becomes a dull repetitive process, until some change or other disrupts it. This hammers the fact of ageing and maturity home to you with the realisation that you are getting a bit too old for some thing or other. The first change for me was when I became a man. All my fantasies of childhood were no more. I took on responsibilities that at the time I did not want or know how to handle. When I became married and had a wife who shared my future, it was enjoyable. Then we had a son. I then took the responsibility of a tiny part of me that was separate, and in whom our futures lay. Yet when the time came to hand them on to my son; may he rest with Allah, I did not want to let them go. You see it meant that I was to change yet again. Then, when my only son was killed in battle against the Israelis, I had to decide whether I could or would, want to revert to my previous lifestyle. My wife and I realised that life had to continue, regardless of the pain and sorrow. We felt it is important to understand that we too are here by the will of god or as we Arabs say Inshallah.'

He took my hand, his was dry yet firm and strong. 'Francis would you now be my son and help me in

my quest? I did not have the time to ask you the
other night and I humbly do so now. ' His candour
and warmth astounded me. 'Why choose me?' I
said. Jibril tightened his grip. 'Francis please do not
question my reason. You should be aware of the
picture on the box. It is of a judgement. There are
signs that the person being judged is from a land far
away from here. You are from far away towards the
North Star. Do not question fate. The signs point to
you.' 'Go on Jibril, it could have been any
European.' I said jokingly, giving a big grin. 'Then
Francis, you had better look at this' He brought out
a box, slightly bigger than the one he had let me
take away that fateful evening. Handing it to Anna,
he looked her right in the eyes and asked her
outright. 'Would you not agree with me too please?'
I saw her face go absolutely white; she sat there
rigid and silent. Passing me the box without saying
a word, Anna found a tissue and wiped her eyes. I
looked at the box, as beautiful as the one I knew; it
was very much the same construction, also with the
ankh key and Uchat lock orifice. I turned it so that I
might see the top. There was a portrait of a
pharaoh, in full regalia. The sheer beauty of his
ornaments of office, the crook and flail were traced
out in the finest gold leaf. The lid was inlaid with
opal and ivory, gold and silver, ruby and topaz. I
had never seen such workmanship in my life. The

detail was like a photograph as before. The face stared back at me from the polished wood. There was certainly no doubt about it. The face gave it all away. Bloody hell what was going on here? I could see why Anna had reacted as she had. The face was mine!

Chap 13

To say I was dumbstruck was the understatement of the millennium. It was as though I had been photographed and the print copied onto this box. I just looked, and the thoughts came racing like a frenetic, formula-one, carbon-fibre composite vehicle, through what I took to be my mind. Was it some gigantic 'You've been framed' hoax? No it certainly wasn't. My own physical condition told me that. I could feel the stitches stinging as my sweat found its way into the wounds. I was certainly not dreaming. What was going on? Perhaps this box was a forgery? Looking at Anna and Jibril, I knew that not to be so. As if in answer to my thoughts Jibril said ' I know this box to be genuine Francis. I have had it examined by experts in Cairo. Yes, I know now that was my error. They had it photographed without my permission and our enemies have known your face all along. They suspect you know too, and have sought you out to lead them to wherever this quest takes us.

Feeling a bit upset and still unsure of the role I was being expected to fill all I could say was 'I just can't understand it. How long have you known that there was a chance that I had been recognised?' I asked no one in particular. Jibril answered me by taking hold of my arm and pulling me towards him. 'Francis, this was the reason I asked you to come to

my house in the first place. I had wanted to be sure
it was your image on the box. I knew you would
return to Egypt when the pieces of the puzzle came
together. My enquiries had made me see this and I
could not believe it either. When I saw you at the
temple I did not know what it meant. I wanted to
tell you immediately, but I just had to be convinced
it was not my imagination. I had intended to speak
with you first before letting you in on my secret.
 It was only when I returned from the mosque that
evening, having learnt of the death of Mamout and
his cousin that I knew something had gone wrong. I
had sent the box via a friend to another
acquaintance in Cairo, so that I might find out
which pharaoh was portrayed there. The age was
not in contention but the identity of the face was.
He was obviously a king because of his clothes, his
crown and the symbols of his office you see there is
no cartouche?' I could see Anna looked slightly
mystified. 'Just a moment Jibril' I turned to explain
the word to Anna 'there was no oblong, round
shape with a line along the bottom and hieroglyphic
writing inside it. That was what Jibril meant. When
the Frenchman Champollion deciphered the Rosetta
stone, he used the French term for little box to
describe the shape that surrounded the name of the
person. That was one of the clues that led to us
being able to read the ancient writing'

I apologised for my interruption, and Jibril
continued.' There is no missing pharaoh in the list
of kings. As far as is known, we have a continuous
list of all the kings. I feel that this one is odd in
many ways. For a start, the quality of the likeness is
extremely fine. It seems so real. The cartouche is not
there; thus we cannot put a name to the face. If it is
a hoax, then why do men kill for it? What do you
think Francis?' I then told Jibril what Anna and I
had deciphered from the papers I had taken from
the dead men. 'Hold on a minute' Said Anna.
'Perhaps the absence of a name is deliberate and we
are being encouraged to fill in the missing portions.
What I feel is that we must continue looking at the
whole thing as though we cannot understand the
writing or the customs of the time and treat it as
though it is a general message to whoever finds it.
Would it make any difference even if we did know
the name of this man?' Both Jibril and I had to agree
with her. Anna went on. 'There are certain things
on the boxes that we all concede, could not be
painted without the use of a lens of some sort. We
know that whoever painted the box knew that
Jupiter has a red spot and four moons. There is a
way to tell longitude by the position and rising of
Jupiter's moons. Could it be trying to let us know
where something is hidden?' 'Good thinking Anna'
I exclaimed, 'that takes care of the Global

Positioning System we've got. Who else knows
what is going on? Someone wanted to borrow the
boxes for a fee, and I shall accentuate the word
borrow. That means that the information is
contained within the items we have. It can be
extracted and the items returned to us. Obviously,
the value rests in the messages hidden within them.
Do the contents of these boxes point towards
something else? If so then what could it be? There is
a hidden clue or clues, all wrapped up in ancient
form with my portrait on the cover. It also means
that there are people out there who know we have
it. They want it too. So what the hell do they want
to do with it?' I was trying to get my mind around
the problem. How did the attackers know where to
go? How did they know it was me who had the
boxes? How were they able to send out two teams
to take the items? Things were becoming a little
clearer. They had been looking for them for a long
time now. They already had agents on the ground,
ready to pounce if reports came up of their or my
whereabouts. I had to know certain facts to enable
me to close the loop of reasoning. The people I
needed were here. I looked towards my
companions. 'Jibril I need you to really think this
out. Did any of your acquaintances in Cairo report
any problems?' He replied after consideration that
there had been no leak of security at all; the

penalties for illicit possession of ancient artefacts were extremely harsh. It was all done in the greatest of secrecy. 'Yet a photograph was taken?' I asked. 'Yes Francis, you have to understand that this took place quite a time ago. Nothing has happened in the meantime. It is possible however, that your arrival started off the process. They may have matched your photograph with the picture on the box.' 'Yes, but that would infer there was input from high places. Does it mean that government officials are involved? I might believe it because of the satellite communications device I found. I am sure you may be on to something. I think we had better try to find out a little more.' Anna said that it was getting too complicated to even assume anything. She touched my arm and suggested we return to the hotel and examine the rest of the boxes. Jibril looked drawn and tired from the constant banter and questions. Both Anna and I had forgotten how ill he was 'What are you going to do now?' He said weakly. 'We will return tomorrow,' I said. 'No my friend, I will not be here tomorrow, I shall send word where I shall be. There is too much danger for us all so we should be careful.' He looked at Anna and gave her the second box. 'I would like you to protect this man. Use all your knowledge to solve the mystery. I shall do all I can to assist you. It is no coincidence that it is his face. I believe history has waited for the

answer.' I looked at them both. I was still perplexed
by all this intrigue, I had no idea what my role was,
other than as an innocent bystander who had fallen
into a pretty scary situation and as I caught Anna's
smile I knew I had fallen in love too.
Leaving Jibril, we made our way carefully back to
the street outside. I looked at the street sign that
said Shari Maabed el Karnak and thought that I
would like to visit the temple complex at Karnak as
I had intended before all this trouble. I resigned
myself to not doing so during this holiday however.
As we walked into the dusty street, the sounds of
the final calling to prayer rang out from the
multitude of mosques that surrounded us. It all
seemed a bit surreal just to be normal for a while,
and not like a piece of a weird jigsaw puzzle of
uncertainty. Neither of us spoke for quite a time.
We both knew that there was no retreat from our
desire to find out, and to follow wherever the clues
led us. I accepted the offer of a passing caleesh of a
ride back to the main square, and after the
obligatory bartering, had agreed the price. We
ascended the well-sprung carriage and were
confronted by a big heart shaped picture frame,
filled with portraits of famous couples, amongst
whom, I saw Hugh Grant, Liz Hurley and Richard
Burton with Liz Taylor. If I had not been with
Anna, I would have thought it pretty tacky. This

was certainly the love bus home. We both examined our conveyance and noticed the tassels around the hood. There was an amulet in the shape of an eye of Horus suspended beside me. I asked the driver why this was so. He turned round, letting the poor horse make its own way down the Corniesh el Nile while he proceeded to tell me how lovers would look through the right eye because it was lucky. The left eye was to see bad things. I had to remind him several times, that we were meandering dangerously close to oncoming traffic. He just grinned, showing me a set of teeth like gravestones as he said. 'Always mister, it is the right eye of the god that is shown in the papyrus pictures and on the temple walls. The soul or Ka needs to know where it is going through the underworld; Horus the hawk knows all things. So it is written.' He returned his concentration to the road ahead as we narrowly avoided a collision with a passing taxi. I then knew that this was the clue for which we had been searching. The eye of the hawk would show the way. I held Anna's hand and gently spoke into her ear. 'I believe we will have to make a visit to Cairo, unless we can find the information we want here. I will let you know what I'm thinking when we get back to the hotel.'

She flashed those enchanting eyes at me, the neon of a shop-sign radiating them an electric blue. 'I don't need to be back at the Joliville to know what you are thinking, I assume I am thinking the same romantic thoughts as you?' The now obligatory giggles started, I was really enjoying these interludes, as they punctuated the reality of our situation, and were all that stopped me from giving up completely.

We looked at the many cruise ships tied up to the moorings on our right; there must have been over fifty of them. I thought that I would like to be just a tourist without the baggage of the small boxes and the beating I had collected. Unfortunately that chance had gone long before this holiday had even begun. My face had led me into this mess and it was a part of me I could not change; in reality, I had been part of this quest from the day I was born. There could be no turning back.

Chap 14

The evening sky was darkening now and the monochromatic mercurial, whitish glow of the streetlamps painted the palm trees a strange tinge of green. I noticed the orange sodium lamps illuminating the temple as we passed it on our left. We were being given the grand tour. The shadows of the lotus columns were cast like multiple fingers against the desert sand. The rhythmic clip clopping of the hooves, along with the general murmur of the traffic, were like a background similar to a hive of bees. I drank it in so that I might perhaps slow down time itself. Her warmth, her sweet smell, her vibrancy, her presence, and most of all her love were changing me from one who might have cared; into one who would not ever stop caring. All too soon, we were at our destination outside the Post Office on Shari el Mahatta not far from where we started and near to the brightly lit souk where I hoped to buy some new clothes. I gently helped Anna down from the carriage, accenting my devotion with a little bow. She smiled and waited whilst I paid our driver and looked a little surprised when I tipped him generously. As we walked away from our now happy coachman, she nudged me and said, 'what did you tell me? Not too generous? You are a big sweet soft person after all.'

'Not so' I said 'that man has solved part of the
problem for us; we must retrieve the bits from the
pool area and have another look at them. I think I
know what to do with the hawk. Come to think of
it, I have never really examined it at all.'
We entered an arcade that seemed new and a bit
more up market than the usual bazaar. I was
pleased to see a multitude of tee shirts, jeans and
trainers all badged, and clones of all the leading
designer labels. I was aware that several people had
given me more than a cursory glance, so I asked
Anna if I was dirty, or smelt, or just looked odd. She
assured me that none of those things were true. I
was thus suspicious that something was not quite
right and we had better be on our guard. We
headed for a large shop with racks of clothes, hats
and shoes placed strategically
The clothing shop was enticing, I could smell
incense burning, and the aromatic myrrh tickled my
olfactory senses and reminded me of my many
years as an altar boy in some far near forgotten part
of my life. We emerged from this emporium of
goodies ten minutes later with at least enough
clothes to start our own boutique. These were paid
for from the wad of dollars I had extracted from the
briefcase. I was constantly aware that we might be
followed, and managed to keep a weather eye open
for that eventuality. I was not surprised to see a

portly man wearing a voluminous galabia striding towards us. He looked like a felucca in full sail as he pushed his way through the crowded pathway. He had been expecting to catch us still in the shop and had not quite made it. 'Hello Khalid, it's a warm night for a jog.' I quipped, noting his face, which was bathed in sweat. 'What brings you rushing' I had no time to continue my facetious remark as he gathered Anna and myself along with numerous carrier bags, and precipitated us, in a flurry of arms, legs, clothing and an adjacent carpet; into a shop doorway. The crashing of glass and the report of automatic fire were like some war movie. People were screaming and running wildly as a motorcycle carrying two men one of whom appeared to be carrying a short-barrelled machine pistol broke through and came towards us. Khalid shouted something and from a half-sitting position, from which his remarkable bulk was giving us cover, let fly two shots from a large handgun. I saw the driver crumple as the hollow rounds tore into him. The motorcycle crashed into a display of brassware beside us and deposited it and the riders in the middle of the pathway. The sound was deafening as the trays, pots, pans and plates skidded and rolled like Frisbees around the rapidly clearing area. Two armed men returned fire from the shops to the left and right of us. The armed pillion rider was up and running to seek anonymity within the mass of people who were now diving for cover. A shot from his left span him into a plate glass window where he died amongst a load of cheap souvenirs and leather bags. His blood pooled on the sidewalk, whilst the shop owner hastily removed as much stock as possible from the mayhem. I had the impression he had seen it all before.

 I turned painfully around as Khalid rolled off my legs Anna lay still. I felt for her pulse, and was relieved to find it working perfectly. I quickly examined her and blessed God she was not wounded. My heart raced as I tried to ascertain the extent of her injuries. She confounded me by sitting up panting and staring frightened all around her. I held her so close; I had no desire to let her go. She had just been winded when Khalid had saved us with that heroic rugby tackle of his. I would not lose her now I knew that I would change my entire life for her. This was the most powerful feeling I had ever experienced. This was really love.

Chap 15

Khalid now took control, issuing orders as he assessed the situation, his command was total and the multiplicity of uniformed police personnel who had appeared in vast numbers from every direction obeyed his every word. The chaos was turning into order as each facet of our attempted murders, was removed.

Our prospective, unsuccessful killers, were extracted, photographed, and bagged up with phenomenal haste along with their motorcycle by concerted effort. I just sat there, pretty winded by Khalid's charge, still propped up against the shattered window frame, hugging Anna to me.

I was finding it a bit difficult to breathe so I moved slightly. I then became aware of a cloying wetness and a stabbing pain under my armpit against my left breast.

Thinking I had rolled onto some glass, I raised my arm to remove whatever splinter had penetrated my clothing. A stream of blood ran down my shirt and onto the marble step. Anna screamed, as she became aware, as I was now, that I had been hit. A police paramedic rammed a field dressing into the wound, packing the bulky object hard to my side and then bound my left arm to my body in an attempt to stop the bleeding. Khalid then picked me

up as though I was a child, and gently carried me at least fifty metres through the bazaar and outside into the street where a White Citroen Estate, which on inspection turned out to be an ambulance was waiting. It was drawn up at the entrance to the bazaar obviously in preparation
. Anna, still suffering from the effects of shock, followed. She was still carrying the carrier bags containing our recent acquisitions, which surprisingly she had appeared not let go of throughout the entire episode. I was amazed how much detail I could take in considering I had just been shot. Time appeared to pass like a snail going uphill.

The tailgate was raised, and Khalid slowly lowered me onto a russet upholstered stretcher. Anna, plus my baggage was crammed into the rear alongside my head, where she constantly entreated me to remain conscious. This was difficult under the circumstances as I was by now haemorrhaging extremely seriously. Her voice seemed to draw my awareness so that it felt like I was drifting.

One of the white suited ambulance men strapped me onto the well-worn surface, and amid a symphony of sirens, we were rushed off to hospital. I vaguely remember them using a second-hand polythene oxygen mask that smelled of stale vomit and without a regulating device, blasting a gale against my face.

I was more concerned that the needles to be used on me were new and sterile than I was about my present predicament. I kept on telling Anna that I had a gold card and priority medical cover. Her tears splashing on my face were the last things I remember.

Those beautiful eyes were again swimming in front of me. My mouth was again, as dry as the bottom of a Saharan sandpit at high noon. I croaked a greeting and promptly passed out again. I was drifting within the confines of a passageway that was inscribed with beautiful words that only I could understand.

There were people carrying me on their shoulders on some type of large stretcher. I seemed to be half in and half out of consciousness. There was background music of a form I had never heard before; it was trendy with an ethereal flute playing the lead. It crossed my mind that I should try and get a recording if possible.

A group of people joined those who were carrying me, they were mournful and started singing dirge-like songs. This broke the auditory effect for me and banished the moment.

I was upset because they had ruined the magic of the music. I was floating again; there was a wonderful smell of perfume and sweetness. I was sure I could hear that music again, it was very relaxing and more beautiful. It must be the effects of the anaesthetic I told myself, as I observed the people around me.

They did not look like doctors in surgical dress; in fact they looked like a fancy dress cavalcade. I distinctly noticed the opulence of their gold ornaments, which scintillated in the soft light. I was inches away from the ceiling of this corridor, and could discern every crack in the extremely white plaster. A voice began to sing a strange song. I attempted to turn my head, so that I might see more of what was going on, but my body was constrained by something. My arms and legs were as though glued to the stretcher.

 The song was repeated time after time and I thought it a bit irreverent and strange that my way to the operating theatre was being treated as some kind of a joke.

I could feel the roughness of my surgical gown on my skin; only it did not look like a surgical gown at all. It seemed to be all bandages. I was sure I had only been hit just once, but I had not felt that either, had I? Attempting to understand the situation I had woken into; I decided to make an attempt to get some idea of how bad a state, my body was in. I

thus took stock of what senses remained to test
those bits I could still feel or see.

Perhaps the shot had cut a nerve? Was I paralysed?
Well I might just as well have been. I couldn't move
a bloody thing. I could still feel sensation of touch,
smell sight and sound. As for taste, that was an
understatement, as my mouth was very salty, as
salty as the Dead Sea.

There were two heavy rod-like items in my hands
that seemed to weigh me down still further. My
head was locked into some sort of helmet that
seemed to weigh a ton or more. Everything was
slightly out of focus, as though the lenses of my
eyes were smeared with grease.

I could see a large group of people, all with fine
clothing. Some of them were crying, and yet some
were singing and playing strange sounding musical
instruments. I was dreaming! I had to be; this was
not an entertaining experience and I hoped it would
end soon. The drugs they were using on me were
certainly having a nasty effect now.

Unfortunately I was not asleep but fully conscious
there was too much tactile input to be just a dream.
This was real and really happening, I was
mummified, going to be interred in some grave or
other. I was beginning to panic, the claustrophobic
retention of the stretcher and whatever garments I

was wearing was constricting my chest and thus, my ability to breathe.

I tried to raise myself to protest but I could not move. I could hear the words 'Isis giver of life bring Geb to his rest. Geb who is your father, the husband of Nut your mother; is slain. May you and your brother Osiris bring retribution upon his killers. Through the right eye of Horus may be seen the future. May Geb go to his rest beyond the stars from which he came. May the gold circles carry the way to his eternal rest. May they guide him back to that place from which he came.'

I seemed to understand what it was they were singing about. It was though the language was new to me, but somewhere, deep in my innermost memories, it was deciphered.

 As the chanting continued, I began to understand still more. My comprehension was returning from the core of my brain. I felt that I had been here before, and I could vaguely remember this place. The writing on the walls was becoming distinct and comprehensible. This must be a hallucination, as I had never set foot in this specific hospital before. The decorations were certainly ethnic art and were to be commended, I thought.

Where were they taking me now? I was incapable of physical movement, so I was entirely at their mercy. I could feel the warmth of the lamps and yet also feel the chill of the adjacent limestone surface inches from my face. The chanting continued 'Hail Geb who is the father of all. May he lie in eternal peace in this sacred place. May his Ka rise to the heavens and return to the place from which he came. If this was not an operation to save me, it must be my funeral. I must be dead. I really was not sure, as far as I knew this was the big one. I had no prior experience; or had I been here before? I did not feel dead; I could think and see, so I must be alive.

I was to be buried alive! I could not let them know that I was not dead. Didn't anybody see that I was still breathing? Where was Anna? Then I saw her. She was dressed in a beautiful evening gown that shimmered in the light as though she had caught the moon within its folds. She was crying and wailing in her grief and did not notice my urgent eye movements.

I could feel myself sweating with the effort of attempting to convey some indication that I was alive. Khalid was also present, his enormous form clad in only a pure white type of kilt with a gold sash. His oiled, light brown skin reflecting the light. He wore a band of gold around his head. In his powerful arms he held a long black pole topped by a large golden hawk. The bird had its talons as though it was holding onto the pole. It was just as

Jibril had described it. I really was going overboard in this dream.

Another man, flanked by several others, stood on a small ornamental box; he had a large fan of ostrich feathers, which he was waving to cool the officiating clergyman who had a face like a jackal and dark piercing eyes. He was wearing a hat the likes of which I had never seen before. I took him to be an orthodox priest with a strange taste in fashion. He was talking to Anna, but he kept on calling her by a different name. I strained my ears to hear it and it became distinctly clear that something was weirdly wrong.

He called her Serqit, and that name brought me to my senses quicker than the Concorde. I remembered my ancient Egyptian history; Serqit was the wife of Horus and the daughter of Ra. She was represented with the head of a woman and the body of a Scorpion. This was stretching the bounds of normality a bit too far. I knew Anna in the biblical sense and it certainly wasn't true. These names were the fabric of mythology and legend. There had to be a logical explanation. I was in some kind of limbo, a place between life and death. I was on my way out of this life and had awoken to see my own funeral. Why then, were the participants dressed up like ancient Egyptians? Why was I being

treated like this? Was I hallucinating? Were they just surgeons trying to save me? Had they failed?
I was amazed at the depth of my perceptions. If this was the way out of this world, then why were my eyes, nose and ears so sensitive so near to the end of my life? Everything was enhanced. The colours and the smallest sounds were open to my senses in a way they had never been when I had been alive. Perhaps I was reborn, or on my way to the other side? In truth I had always wondered what the actual moment would be like. The only regret I had at this time was that I had finally found a woman who genuinely loved me for myself, and whom I too genuinely loved with all my heart. This caused me great anguish as I lay there waiting for the final minutes of my life to pass into eternity.
I was slipping deeper into the nadir of life, where the delicate balance between the domains of Ra and Osiris crossed. I remembered the picture on the box, the first box I had held. It was the judgement of Thoth, where the heart of the dead individual was balanced against the feather of truth. Would my heart be judged so?
I have not lived a pure and good life, I thought. Would my soul be forced to roam the underworld? Would it do so after the heart was fed to the crocodile? Or would it join Ra on the solar barge to shine forever among the stars?

At this specific moment, either option was unexciting. I was not ready to die just yet. I needed to experience the warmth of true love and the joy of growing old with my soul mate. I could not bear her grief for me for all eternity. If I were to die, it would not be now. I would not let it happen.
I made this resolve with as much strength as my situation allowed. As I did so, the people who were carrying me started to place me down onto a red granite sarcophagus-like table. I was now on a level, where I could see their faces, instead of being carried on the shoulders of my porters. As they turned towards me I was aware of the gold and black striped head coverings with the royal seal embossed on the gold pins that held them together. I still could not see a cartouche. So who was the funeral for? I would not let it be for me.
What is the power of true love? I will never doubt again the inner strength it gave me. I felt the anger and frustration building up within me, until it was like an iceberg sliding towards a super-tanker. The annoyance towards death was born of love, or the desire to prolong that love, now that I had found it. I could not, and damn well would not, release this feeling I had discovered. I was not going to let myself die.
The priest approached me with an iron implement shaped like a small hook with a long handle. I knew

he was going to perform the ceremony of the
opening of the mouth. This was always done to the
mummy prior to burial. It allowed the soul or Ka to
enter the body in preparation for its journey to the
hereafter. I made up my mind that I was not about
to be buried, if I could help it. I could see his mask;
he was portraying Anubis the jackal.

 With a supreme effort, fuelled by my love for
Anna, I sat bolt upright on the table. He visibly
paled and fell gibbering on to his knees, pointing at
me in horror. His acolytes struggled to lift him up,
looking at me in fearful surprise as they did.

There was pandemonium, items fell clattering to the
floor people screamed and the looks on some of the
faces will sustain my wicked sense of humour for
all time. 'He is alive Inshallah'

Arms held me and gently lowered me down to a
prone position. Soothing words told me that I must
keep still and not disturb the wound as I had lost a
lot of blood. I was back and I must not forget the
things I had learned. I had endured the judgement
of Thoth as the second box showed. I would solve
this quest.

Anna was there yet again when I left the twilight
world and came back to ours. Khalid was also
waiting for my return. He had certainly saved our
lives through his prompt action and should be
thanked. I attempted to shake his hand, but only

succeeded in making a groaning noise, as I appeared to be clutching his arm. He seemed to understand whatever look I was giving him. He took my hand and placed it in Anna's. 'Francis' He said quietly. 'You must help me to find the truth. I do not expect you to be able now, not until you are stronger. You are still in danger. I can help, only if I know. Please tell me about the search you are engaged in Francis. Or should I call you Geb?

Chap16

Hearing that name, and its use to address me, was uncanny. I was still under the spell of whatever the experience of the previous few hours had taught me. I had been called Geb, both then and now. Was then in a past life? Why did he call me that, now? How did Khalid know? Did I talk in the operating theatre? No I could not even move a muscle at that time. I had been totally paralysed. I definitely had not uttered a single word. The staff must have been trying to resuscitate me when I suddenly responded, and scared the proverbial out of them. A man in a white coat came with a hypodermic syringe in a dish to administer something. He spoke to Anna and Khalid who moved to let him approach me. I knew his face from somewhere. He had been in my dream too. He had held the fan. How could I dream of someone who I had never seen before? Why did I recognise him? Worse still, why did I fear him? Feeling too weak to protest too much, I caught Khalid's eye and showed my doubt. He picked the man up and literally turned him upside down in a single flowing movement. The syringe and dish fell noisily to the floor along with a handgun. The man struggled and Khalid, who was by now, holding him by the ankles, just dropped him on his head. With a gasp like a deflating football, he flopped, unconscious and lay still.

'Thank you' I gasped and passed out.

I have never slept so much in all my life, whether it was induced through the bash on the head, the bullet in my chest or the loss of blood. I had never been through so many traumas in so short a time. I certainly knew that I had no desire to offer a repeat performance.

When I finally woke up, I decided to come out into the open with Khalid, who by now I knew to be the best friend a man in my position could have. Except Anna, that is. She and I were more than friends were, so I knew what I meant anyway.

The day was already half gone, or as far as I could tell. I did not know where the sun had risen, or even if I was still in the same room as before. I attempted to get up; only to collapse back on the bed as my head did an impression of a carrousel. The noise I made brought an armed policeman into the room, whom after appraising my wakefulness with a slight smile, went out and returned promptly bearing a walkie-talkie. He chatted into the device and I heard the hissing noise as the squelch lifted and an answering voice giving instructions in Arabic.

He stood to attention as though the owner of the voice was in the room. The call finished, he came

and sat down just inside the door, having brought
his chair in with him. He called to another person
outside who went and brought a medical orderly
with insignia on his white coat, I then realised he
was an army medic. I was in a military hospital. He
smiled at me and asked if I felt better, I was
subjected to pulse, temperature and respiration
checks, and then left alone to recover my wits.
A short while later, an officer, in fatigue gear,
entered. My guard was like a cruise missile ejecting
from its launch pod. He shot to his feet so fast; I
could almost smell the soles of his shoes burning.
Having saluted almost hard enough to knock his
own head off, he jabbered away as though he was
recounting my whole life history.
The officer kept looking at me as though convincing
himself that what he was being told was true. I
knew from his insignia that he was a high ranker
but I was unsure how high. I noticed his alert
expression, he radiated power and intelligence, and
his eyes missed nothing. He had very strong
features; his face was agile with a sense of
authority. I supposed him to be in his mid forties,
give or take a few years. By his Mediterranean
appearance I thought him to be from northern
Egypt, probably Alexandria or Cairo. Nodding to
the guard, he dismissed him and waited until he
had left before addressing me in a conspiratorial

tone. 'Welcome to the Mogammu Military Hospital Mr Francis. I hope your stay will bring you health. I am General Imir Hamza, and I am at your service. I will tell you a little of your injury. You received a hit from a nine millimetre round, we assume it was a ricochet as the full bullet did not enter but a sizeable part entered your side and glanced along your ribcage, coming to rest in your pectoral muscle. Unfortunately for you, it severed an artery on its way. It was that which nearly killed you. We have removed the pieces of the bullet and you should be well very soon. So you see the wound was superficial but the blood-loss critical. '
I could not believe that I would merit the attention of a full General. I asked him why I was in a military hospital and not a civilian clinic. 'You are more famous than is safe for you. The police asked for assistance in protecting you. We feel that the several attempts on your life and the troubles that you may be involved in are an attempt to destabilise the whole of Egypt. We have many enemies in the world. Owing to the strategic situation of Egypt, our President and his desire for peace with Israel and our perennial attempts for Arab stability, we are at risk from terrorists at all times'
'What gives you that impression?' I asked him. 'In truth Mr Edwards, there is a plot to assassinate the

President and to turn this country into a
fundamentalist state. This has been going on for
many years now. You will recall the attempts to
destroy our tourist industry and thus bankrupt the
country by simply attacking foreigners and killing a
few. We are just recovering and cannot endure the
financial strain much longer. There is also a more
evil group of individuals who are trying to get their
hands on an atomic weapon. This they hope to buy
from the Russian Mafia, with the proceeds from an
as yet undiscovered tomb.'
I looked at him, the comprehension of the moment,
just gradually turned back the veil of my inability to
understand why all this was happening. The pieces
of the puzzle began to swim into position like a
shoal of tropical fish. The truth was very logical and
very disconcerting. There was more than avarice in
the motive of my attackers. There could be more
than one side after the goodies. One team to get the
clues and find the treasure, and another contrary
team to wipe out any route to it, namely me!
I was the route, and the road works were not
remedial. The journey had certainly not been a
pleasant one so far. Apart from Anna, there had
been little to enjoy along the way.
As if in answer to my thoughts, she swept in to the
room. Her smile would have disarmed the entire
Egyptian army. Khalid followed; he was carrying

the clothes we had bought moments before this latest near fatal episode. His grin was enormous; he was genuine in his joy to see me much recovered. Anna took over, she grasped the Generals hands and she blessed him for his kindness. I could see she was weaving her spell on him as well. He wilted under her gaze and agreed to all she suggested. I thought if only his army could see him now, so human in his reaction, I distinctly felt that I could grow to like him. I was not sure however how hard a man he could be but I assumed to be a General, you had to be a bit mean. He obviously seemed to enjoy the power of rank but he had the right to benefit from his uniform. His clothing was exemplary, with everything in place. I thus thought him a man of precision. Anna however could disarm him with her smile.

Anna sat beside me. She fretted over my hair and gave me a big kiss. Holding my right hand in both of hers, she looked me over. I could see the repressed strain and remnants of tearful hours etched in her eyes. 'Francis, we must get help, I have suggested to Khalid that there may be more we can do. In fact I have told him we will help solve this mystery.' I nodded and addressed our two friends present

' Gentlemen, I had a dream that may be the clue to what we seek.' After recounting the last twenty-

four hours, and being notified that it had actually
been three days. They all were keen to point out
that I had been in a coma and had been transferred
to this hospital for my own safety, after the final
attempt on my life in the last hospital. I said that I
was aware of the move but not of the time that had
passed. Trying hard to take in this update and its
significance, I proceeded to enlighten everyone
including Anna about what I took to be the reason
for the presentation of the numerous boxes.
' There are three boxes. The outer box shows a
portrait of an individual, a Pharaoh, who
regrettably looks like me. Another box with the
judgement of Thoth fits beautifully inside. On that
box are certain clues that let the observer know that
there is more to it than literally meets the eye. In
fact it is the Uchat or the right eye of Horus that will
show us where the treasure is hidden. Inside this
box is another, made of a different material. Inside
that box, is the statue of Horus. He has one eye
missing, and I bet it is the left eye.'
Anna nodded, 'that is right Francis; we have been
examining the contents to see where they lead. So
far we have learnt nothing new. By the way, where
did you hide the box with the picture?' I quickly
told her and Khalid sent one of his men to recover
it. 'Checkmate Francis, why the white king?' I was
quick to point out that had anything fatal happened

to me, it would have been possible to deduce where I might have hidden a part of a king's treasure. I recounted the comments of the caleesh driver and the incantation I had heard in my dream. 'They called me Geb, and so did you Khalid, can you tell me why?' 'That is simple Francis; I have had that dream too. In fact I have had that dream many times. That is why I was so persistent in my chasing you for information. You see I knew you were not being totally honest with me. I am sure we met in a past life.'

' I am not sure that I believe in that sort of thing, but my dream was as real as now.' I said pensively. 'In fact I am not sure it was a dream at all. I saw people. I saw you Khalid, as real and as large as now. I also saw that man who came into the room. Did I say anything when I was going to theatre?' Khalid laughed; his great smile was infectious. It radiated both harmony and empathy. 'No Francis, you could not say anything. You were pronounced dead on arrival at the hospital.' His large hand stilled my surprise and held back my shock. 'I was there when you sat up on the trolley when they came to take you to the mortuary. I shall never forget half the staff in casualty running out of the room, followed by two of my men, dropping everything as they went. You realise that you gave them a severe fright. I have never laughed so much

in my entire life. I had you rushed into theatre then
and they removed two bullets from your chest. As
for the man who tried to kill you in the hospital, he
is assisting me with my enquiries. Not willingly at
the moment, but as time goes on, he will come to
see things my way.' It gave me a chill the way he
said the word my, but desperate times breed
desperate minds. It couldn't be easy in any culture
to get truthful answers from recalcitrant assassins.
I was really hungry; and conveyed this fact to all
present. A few commands later, this was partially
alleviated by a tasty meal of grilled lamb with
potatoes and local green salad. I wolfed it down
with little ceremony and realised halfway through
that I must be a spectacle, due to my haste. I tried to
show contrition, but they all were so glad to have
me back, that they told me I would be forgiven
anything at present. Finally I was satisfied, so the
conversation continued, in order we might make
something of the information in our possession.
A video camera was set upon a tripod to my right,
and the dialogue was committed to history. First of
all, Khalid went on record to assure us both that we
were not under any threat from any of our previous
unwillingness to provide assistance. In fact, he
made it quite clear that our actions were to be
construed as self-preservation.

Anna continued the dialogue with a potted history of the approximate age of the artefacts as far as the constellations were concerned. She also added the information about the view of Jupiter and its moons. All through her explanations the general took notes and nodded at the occasional revelation. I added details as they came to me. My memory was still running in slow motion as I constantly had flashbacks to my premature burial. Every now and again, I would be projected back in time to a vaguely familiar feeling of absolute power. It certainly felt strange, as I have never been much of a megalomaniac; I have always been content to accept life's ups and downs, except where I could change things for the better. I put it down to my recent tribulations. I could not help the violence of each successive return, to the tomb, or wherever it was I was going inside my skull. The various persons, who had been present there, were becoming more familiar. What the hell was going on inside my poor aching head? I felt very strange and whatever it was that I was experiencing, started to take over my consciousness more and more, Noticing my distress, my friends were alarmed, especially as I now started talking in a voice which was certainly not my own. I tried to tell them what was going on, but they just looked at me with incredulity written all over their faces. Everything I said made sense to me, but as it came out of my mouth, even I could not believe how it sounded. Khalid simply smiled and said something to the general. Anna turned to me and pleaded with those beautiful eyes. I assumed she was desirous for the real me to return. She gently held me while I bantered on; her tears were warm on the side of my face as her grief spilled over me. I felt I was slipping away again, but another part of me was growing stronger at the same time.

This experience was mind blowing, but I would not recommend it to anyone. Whilst all this was happening, I could hear that blasted chant somewhere in the inner recesses of my mind. I began to chant it myself, much to my own embarrassment. I felt as though I had committed a stupid faux pas and was embarrassed still more. 'Hail Geb, father of all, return from where you came. Return to your home in the stars. We shall avenge you murder. We shall pass on your creed. Father of Isis and Osiris, may your Ka pass into the next world' I suddenly snapped out of this bad trip. It had to be the medication I thought, except that the chanting continued. I opened my eyes and swore to myself. All those present with me were continuing to sing the words. They poured out fluently and harmoniously like a wonderful hymn from a great choir. I observed Anna, Khalid and

Imir as they clearly spoke the ancient words I had
heard in the hospital. How could this be? Was it a
figment of my imagination after all? They just
looked glassy eyed into the distance and were really
speaking those words I had heard in my dream. We
were all going mad. What was the power of this
box? What was it doing to us?

Chap 17

As the chanting continued, I noticed that aromatic
smell again. It was, or seemed to be a combination
of spices and incense. It filled the senses with an
erotic buzz, and heightened the ability to perceive
colours. My tactile senses were increased; I could
feel every little touch upon my skin all over. I felt
the beads of perspiration pour out of me. The
sensation of each tiny drop moving down my skin
was almost painful.

The slightest movement of the air was like a Jacuzzi
pounding my flesh. Even the buzz of an insect
against the window glass was like a chainsaw. With
my heart beating at the rhythm of the song, I looked
around me. The room seemed to have grown to
enormous proportions and appeared to stretch with
every beat.

Anna and Khalid were staring around as though a
ghost had just walked past. I was then aware that
my companions were caught up in the same
experience as myself.

I was finding it difficult to think. Every little
thought had to be forced out of my aching brain.
Memories of events and ceremonies unfolded with
a reality that was able to cut right through my soul.
I felt the emotion of each as it came. I was sure that I
had not experienced personally any of these, but

still they came and settled in my brain. It was as though a film was being projected into my mind. There was a difference however, the emotion, thoughts, anger and decisions were all my own. I was controlling the events, but I was unable to control the order in which they entered my tired head. Reality was turning upside down. A force far stronger than any I had ever known was running through me. It was as though I knew the story, but I was now having my memory refreshed by an external computer. This was an enforced deja vu and I was unsure if I liked it or not. If it was myself alone, then why was it affecting others? Who or what was really in control?

A few days ago, I had been a reasonably normal person, a bundle of experience, pain, love and expectation. I had really looked forward to this trip. I now became aware that I was becoming two people, Francis Edwards the Man, and Geb the God King. It began to strike me as quite funny, because this would give any psychiatrist a run for his money. I was certainly not a schizophrenic, because this was not self-delusion, others were affected also. I had not flipped but I felt I was tilted.

There had been too many hurts on this route already; I seemed to be the key to what was going on. It was becoming clearer to me now. I still

needed to put everything into some form of
perspective.

As Geb, I had the power to control, but would it
end up controlling me? I began to wonder if I could
use the power of Geb to find out what was shaping
our lives. It seemed that there had been something
waiting for thousands of years to emerge. Like the
genie in the bottle .it had just succeeded and I was
Sinbad. It was involving others outside of my
cognitive sphere in some gigantic battle. The other
persons, whom I did not know personally, actually
knew me. How could that happen? They had tried,
and still were, trying to kill me. I did have some
vague recollection of past enemies, and from deep
inside me there was a faint and distant memory of a
terrific power struggle in which I had been beaten. I
was certainly not a winner at present. I had not lost
yet, not this specific battle.

I felt at that moment, the knowledge that this time,
it was to be to the death. I was to be victor or
vanquished, sacrificed upon the altar of history
come what may. The prospect was not entirely
delightful or welcome, especially the way I was
feeling right now.

Silence descended like a fog within the room. I
looked into the blank faces of three other intelligent
people to whom I trusted and owed my life. They
were looking at me with eyes that showed their

awareness of what had transpired. I prayed that the camera had recorded the events too. I hoped that we might learn what was going on. I noticed the aroma had left, and with it, the peeling back of time. I still knew all that had been placed or awakened in my mind. That part was now indelibly locked into my being. I was now able to transpose myself into the persona, man or king, just as I wished. Praying that I would always be in control, I became Francis again. I spoke to my friends

'Hi folks, did you feel that?' I said with a joke type voice that I did not quite believe came from within myself. My words had the desired effect though, and brightness filled all three pairs of eyes as I glanced from one to the other.

I was not sure how aware they were of the events that had just transpired. 'Did you see that?' I said looking as calm as I could. Anna replied reflectively. 'We were all in a big room, there were many different smells, and you Francis, were sitting in front of us on a beautiful throne with leopard skins and ostrich feathers all around it. You were dressed just like your picture and covered in golden ornaments. You were a pharaoh!' Both Khalid and Imir nodded their assent. 'So I didn't dream it then?' I said with some relief. 'Thank God for that. I thought I was going mad at one point.'

Imir rose and went over to the tripod and now
turned the camera so that we were framed more
centrally in his viewfinder. He rejoined us and
shaking slightly in anticipation and from the effects
of our experience, he began to try to analyse the
event. 'Francis, have you any idea what is going on?
Do you have any idea where the tomb is? Or at
least can you lead us there?'
I looked him squarely in the eyes and pulling
myself up so that I might be more level with him, I
replied that I felt a victim rather than a controller at
this time and yes I was more able to try and explain
although it was extremely unbelievable.
'I wish I could trust and believe in what is
happening to us. ' I said.
Imir replied 'Egypt has always been a spiritual and
mysterious place, all of us are aware of the great
and profound changes that are occurring all over
the world. We have seen the fall of many empires in
the last few years and the power vacuums that have
ensued.' Khalid nodded his assent and continued.
'There is however, a power that has been waiting to
fill the gaps left when the old despotic and evil
regimes of communism and apartheid were
overturned. It is this dark power that has caught us
in its grip of darkness. There are many men that use
the words of the Koran, to fire the hearts of others
to do evil. The holy book does not preach bad

things. It is like your bible but meant to be understood and obeyed by everyone. So that people could live together in peace. Yet it was our Arab culture that gave the world the beauty of logic, rhetoric and astronomy when your cultures were living in total ignorance and unable to even write their own language. We do however share the fear of the return of Shaitan or as you Christians call him, Satan. So our history is written from the dawn of time. Our cultures share the stories in many ways. That there has been and will be a great battle of good against evil. That our ancestors spoke to God, that there are divine beings, which we call angels, and that there have been humans who possess the power of prophecy.
Men have fought and died for their opinions of God and yet there has always been the common doctrine of brotherly love, charity and kindness that God demanded, and they ignored in his name, just to suit their own politics. Your history does not even record the arrival of our prophet except as an interesting event. In fact your culture did not have a proper written language until much later.'
Inwardly I thought that this was a profound statement from a policeman. There had to be more to this man than just his size.
We all nodded and then Khalid and Anna both looked at me 'It is about time you explained

Francis' said Anna. 'Wasn't I in the process of trying to explain the boxes before this happened?' I asked.

It was at that point that the logic of the events started to become clear, it was not too difficult to comprehend if certain facts were taken into consideration. 'What I have to say now will seem obvious, but it will open our eyes to the real purpose of things' I went on reflectively.

' A thought came to me several days ago when I was at Medinet Habu but I did not realise the significance of it at the time. All through the history of mankind, there has been a communion with a superior power that was not from this world but from beyond. Did our ancestors see this power? Did they try to pass on the experience of knowing or seeing what may have been the most important event to touch mankind? Did they tell or record a story of whatever it was? Has that story been distorted by time, and telling? However has the core of the story remained intact?

I think it has. What we see today, is four thousand years of evolution of that story, superimposed one upon the other; by subsequent conquering cultures that each absorbed parts of it. Was that power ever understood or used? Or did it become myth and legend?

When those that had actually experienced the visitation or whatever you like to call it had passed on, were there records of the event? I am sure there would have been. Someone would have recorded it in whatever way was at his or her disposal. We have the Bible and Koran to back up that theory. The New Testament is evidence that someone thought that there had been a mysterious event worthy of record. In fact several records exist to prove that a person of great significance had lived and died.'

I looked at my companions and they encouraged me to continue.

'There has always been a mystique about the culture of ancient Egypt and its effect upon the civilisations, which first conquered it, copied it and then followed it. Why did they do it? I feel that by the logic of the time, such great monuments could not be destroyed easily. Thus the memory or story should pass through each succeeding generation. These people, your ancestors Khalid and Imir, knew things that we have yet to rediscover. The effect on subsequent generations is still profound.

To this day, visitors are fascinated by the sheer physical size of the parts that went to build the various temples and statues, let alone the technology that designed, worshiped, ran and constructed the buildings themselves. The people, who conceived and used these temples, did so for a reason that I, in my search for understanding, am beginning to experience for myself.

The presence of the architects and the kings, who commissioned their design, was still upon the face of the earth. They could still control the minds of generations spaced thousands of years apart. I thought that it was the ancient equivalent of a recording in stone that was replayed every time a person gazed upon the sheer beauty and absolute sympathy of the design and positioning. Just look at the carvings and statues that remain around here alone.

The buildings were their version of our computer CD-ROM's. All data was stored in, or upon them. Their size made it difficult to bury or destroy. We have only miniaturised the method; the message was the same. It was historical data that measured the existence of certain people. They served to make us think about them long after their death. They could not be forgotten.

The reason of their existence was the same ambition that man has had for time immemorial, to live for all eternity. '

'It looks as though they have succeeded so far,' said Anna.

Khalid and Imir nodded assent.

'Please continue Francis ' Anna said, and as I tried
    to continue she mouthed silently 'I love you too'
It was taken aback by this admission and thus
stumbled to bring my mind back to my thoughts.
'How much is myth?' I continued. ' I wish I could
guess accurately, but there is so much we are just
beginning to find out and understand.
Some of the stories have been proven such as Troy
and Zimbabwe being great cities. Yet until as
recently as 1872 until the German archaeologist
Heinrich Schielmann believed in the stories of
Homer, Troy was thought to be a myth. There had
been a pre-Hellenic culture, around 2800 BC, which
had preceded Plato, Pythagoras and Aristotle
whom we still respect today. You see; we use those
things that are useful and tend to ignore others,
which we do not find as interesting. Thus there
were contemporaries to the ancient Egyptian Kings.
They obviously knew that each other existed and
even swapped cultures. See how many similar
stories exist in Greek mythology and Egypt
concerning the Gods and the trouble they caused.
We seem to think that they were without scientific
knowledge. However they did things on such a
large scale, that many think they needed extra
terrestrial input .To be truthful. I still have some
reservations, but the moons depicted on the box
tend to sway me a little in that direction. The

miniaturisation and the need of a lens to produce the details, is obviously a message from down the centuries or an elaborate hoax.

Our experiences recently dictate that hypothesis to be untrue. We must therefore take this thing as fact. I would call the monuments sentiments in stone, and the boxes messages in miniature. I still do not believe what I am experiencing, but I must assume that it is logical and that I am not going mad. I know that virtually everyone prays at some time in their lives and apparently talks to a Supreme Being, or themselves, in order to obtain some spiritual assistance or intervention. They even build churches, mosques and temples, so that they can do it together, as if they believe that a combined effort will increase the power of prayer.

We all believe in something or at least feel the need to do so with few exceptions. Even confirmed atheists will have doubts, or mourn the passing of a friend. Why has mankind felt the need to put flowers on graves or even talk to the dead through spiritualists?

All this thought has convinced me that whatever it is that has enveloped us in its mystery has a purpose and that we would be wrong to ignore our responsibilities as they unfold. Now there is a definite course of action to take. We are looking for something exceptional, which has great value and importance. I am not sure exactly what it is but I feel the boxes and the contents are the route to a solution. I also feel that we will soon be finding out exactly what it all means'

Chap 18

Whilst delivering my explanation, I took the falcon
from its ivory box. 'Jibril was so right, this is
fantastic'. Turning it to the light I noticed a slight
protuberance at the rear. This seemed so out of
place with the exquisite workmanship of the statue.
I wondered if there might be another piece to which
this attached. It could just be a tiny hook. Looking
into the final box, the only other pieces were the
little circular earring type ornaments; there was
nothing else, which came with the falcon. Could
these hang on the back? What would be the
purpose of it anyway?

Suddenly it all became clear. What were the boxes
telling us? The outer box said 'Hey it's you Francis.'
The second box said that there is a judgement of
good against evil and that looking through a
precision lens will reveal all. A lens! Yes damn it a
lens! Through the right eye of Horus will come the
truth? It was simple but also elegant. Why had I not
seen it earlier? But the eye was broken so perhaps
the thing might not now work.

I took a disc out of the box, and with a little care
was able to hang it on the tiny hook. Lifting the
statue to my eye, I looked at it through the cracked
clear jewel that served there. I saw three little
images similar to a reflection in a broken mirror but

instead of being fragmented, they were coherent.
The lens was acting like a kaleidoscope toy,
splitting and refracting the light joining the
previously illegible lines into proper form. Thus
when observed in this manner, these made up a
letter or number; and by turning the disc around on
its hook bearing, one was able to spell out a
message, letter by letter. It was a way of looking at
three separate areas of the disc surface all
superimposed on my retina to form an image,
which now made sense. It was a remarkable way of
keeping secret whatever was written there. This
was truly a fantastic piece of engineering to encrypt
whatever message was recorded on the discs.
To the uninformed observer, the discs could not be
interpreted even using a microscope as the
individual parts of the writing were not seen
together with the correct orientation, except
through this high precision lens system.
The writing was unknown to me but something in
my subconscious let me read it. In my excitement I
had forgotten that I was not conveying my findings
to my companions. Apologising for my oversight, I
quickly explained what I had found, and pleading
for a little peace to try and translate the writing, I
commenced to read aloud. 'These are numbers in
groups of twos, there are two sets of three groups.'

Imir quickly came back with the possibility of them being co-ordinates on a map. 'Let us find out if this is so Francis' he spoke into his portable radio and a commotion was heard outside. Quickly a globe was produced, and placed on a table near me. As I read out the numbers, it was obvious that the precision of these placed the indicated point nowhere near land at all. 'It cannot be so I am afraid. They must mean something else.' Said Anna. 'Hold on a minute ' she continued 'we have a bit of a problem not with latitude, but with longitude. Since latitude is fixed from the angle of the sun in the sky at a specific time of day and by night the elevation of the pole star, it can vary only from two fixed points on the planet; I mean the poles relative to the equator. It can be calculated very easily using a sextant by day and with an astrolabe against the stars at night. We know that the information was known thousands of years ago. It could therefore have been measured and recorded. How about drawing a line around the globe to see where it touches land?'

At her suggestion, three other pairs of hands attempted to turn the globe, tracing the latitude across its surface. ' Remember that it was only a relatively short time ago that Greenwich was designated as zero longitude.' Anna continued 'until then, there was no way to calculate it, and only by estimation, could you even attempt to find out how far into the voyage you might be. What we are doing now is to extrapolate the line to see if it comes anywhere near Egypt.'

We turned the globe, Anna keeping her finger at the approximate level of the latitude. Sure enough, the line ran right across the giant bend in the Nile at Luxor. 'The chances are that it is on the West Bank, towards the setting sun.' She said confidently and continued almost euphorically. 'How do we find the longitude? Well that is easy, as I have explained to Francis before. We can calculate it from the picture. 'What do you mean?' said Khalid in awe. I looked at Anna; she was truly radiant in her enthusiasm, with sparkling eyes and a vivaciousness that defied the anguish and pain she had obviously been through on my behalf. I thanked all that I held holy that we had met and fallen in love. I was so proud that she had chosen me, and of her obvious contribution to solving this mystery.

'That is easy, we look at the moons of Jupiter and by their rising we can calculate the longitude. We do not need Greenwich for this because the accurate measurement of longitude was unknown before the invention of an accurate clock and there was no zero datum line before Greenwich.

We therefore use a sidereal datum. By that I mean
we get our datum from space. That would have
been the way the ancient Egyptians did it. Their
figure of longitude is useless to us but when we
calculate the exact point, we will have an interesting
insight to their version of the position of the place
we seek.'
Both Khalid and Imir looked in awe at this beautiful
lady who had won their hearts also and virtually
fell over each other to understand her reasoning. ' It
is obvious to me' she continued, 'that we all fit
together as a team, both now and possibly as before
in our past lives. I am sure that this was meant to
be'
This seemed to be the obvious answer to the bond
that existed between all of us. For such a group to
assemble in such a short time and really care about
each other as much as we obviously did was much
more than a coincidence. In fact it was more like a
miracle. Anna finished her outpouring with a
promise that she would show us how to work out
the longitude from the moons of Jupiter after I had
deciphered the discs.
I changed the disc and there was writing there, I
spoke the words out loud, not sure of what they
actually meant as the lack of context put me off
track. I realised that I was reading them out of
sequence and the wrong order. There were as many

discs as slots, so I was thankful that none seemed to be missing. After a little experimentation, I found that if they were orientated in a certain way, a number was visible. I laughingly explained my findings. One by one I extracted them from the last box and laid them beside me as I put the various discs in order.

Putting the first into the priceless viewer, I began to read.' Hail Geb, it is from time that you return. Many of your sons have gone on into eternity. The world is blessed again by your Ka. Your Ba now walks the temples of this land.'

I changed the disc and turned the second one around to continue. 'Beware! Your enemies once more have gathered in this place to destroy all you left. The power they have is much mightier than before. They feel the need to turn the desert into glass and the cities into fire and dust.' I changed again, fumbling in my haste to read this prophetic missive. 'This time you must destroy them. They shall turn whole countries against you. They shall seek to destroy you by any means. Do not fail us. We have set down a place for you that shall repel all our enemies. We have left you mighty power where the boat of Ra enters the sky. Ra in his heavens shall be your ally.'

I changed again and continued. 'Horus shall show you the secret place. Beware! Only you may enter for it has been made for you alone.' I stopped here, because a feeling of great sadness swept over me. I felt that I had known the writer of these words, for they were more than words to me.

Pulling myself together, I looked at those around me who were willing me to continue my narrative 'Nations shall perish under the new order. They must be not allowed to steal the power of Ra. He is mighty, but his power now sleeps with his sons in the west. From the north you must come. When the moon is shown through the eye and at the appointed hour'

Another change of disc, this was getting excitingly complicated. 'The temple gates shall be open to you. One will come unto you, he is already known to you. Together you will commence the fight.'

I changed another disc but could not help thinking why so complicated? Starting again I read. ' You shall see the hand of Ra. Touch it not. Wait until he rises to show the place where you may hold his hand. Do not fear him. He will lead you unto his house. You will put on his sword and shield, and with his crown; you shall become Geb again'.

I found a symbol that I did not instinctively know and stopped for a moment. To try and make sense, I scanned forward a little to get the next words and was thus silent. Reading the following message I was shaken. It said simply Beware! Your enemy is with you always and is one you care about. He one you might not kill. I paused here to take in the sheer magnitude of the ancient message. Sometimes it is difficult to get an exact meaning of what you are reading. The ancient language had no punctuation or expression marks; thus things could be ambiguous and as I was unsure of what the writer intended to tell me, I had my doubts. It is extremely difficult to understand what had been written thousands of years ago and in a language few understood. I struggled to get the meaning but the present circumstances with my companions to choose from, limited my options. I hoped it could not be Anna for she was extremely close to me but I would have to reserve judgement until I knew better.

As Francis I was not quite sure I was even myself. As Geb I was still a mixed up individual with vague memories of a long forgotten past which I could read about but not understand the meanings in the texts on the discs. Who was the enemy? Was it wise to continue this? Was it right to be recording this for others to see? As Francis, I had to think. It was going to be exceedingly difficult from now on to do anything, if a record of my narrative was leaked, giving our plans away to others.

What before, had seemed a good idea, could now spell disaster. If things were that powerful, then as

the prime controller, I should exercise more control.
Perhaps I should release a few red herrings to
confuse friend and foe alike.
I made a show of tiredness and changed the disc. It
would not do to let anyone know of the warning
contained on the last one. Did it mean that someone
here was my enemy? I prayed it was not so, with all
my heart because I felt love for all three, a love of
having known them for all my life, or so it seemed.
Then we were different, now is just a continuation
of then. Obviously there is a continuum if you are
immortal. The only thing you do not do is die
forever. You experience the process of physical
death but not the normal eternal death. You are reborn at the earliest convenience with your
conscious memories erased or at least put into
background mode. I wondered if that was to protect
you from those who brought you up. For they
would truly fear you if you were to exhibit
knowledgeable traits whilst you were so young and
vulnerable. I decided it would be better for them
not to know until you chose the right moment to tell
them. That brought me to question at what time is it
best for you to know? Let me assure you that I
doubt that I would ever come to terms with the
implication, let alone the truth of my personal
history. It does raise some interesting questions
however. Why me? What is the point? Now that is a

good one. Do I really believe it? Well I am just going to have to live with it then. Was Anna also like me? Could our love be really that good? I must stop this exercise as all I am doing is giving myself the problem of finding loads of answers.

It was a true love for Anna, a fraternal love for Khalid and a growing friendship for Imir.

Anna had been instrumental in my growing awareness of my other self. She had been emotionally

touched, and had shown real pain as she suffered as well.

Khalid had saved my life on more than one occasion, even risking his own in the process.

Imir was my benefactor; he was a powerful man who believed in me. He could control many on my behalf, or his own for that matter. He was after all a servant of the state and could be working for another power. I decided that I would not let myself get paranoid about it but wait and see.

Chap19

Anna broke into my thoughts, her sweet voice silencing all doubts I held previously.

'Now let us try to work out the longitude of our mystery place. First of all let me explain how our ancient mariners and explorers found their way by the stars.

It is easy to see your latitude by using the sun. Just compare the angle of the sun above the horizon when it is at its highest point, in other words at noon or its meridian. Look up the exact angle in a table because you need to know where it should be at that time of year and simply calculate where you are.

After the invention of the telescope, astronomers noticed that our planets also had moons. They also saw that there was a pattern in the orbits. This pattern could be used to navigate.

Jupiter is rather interesting. There is a way to get an approximate value of longitude if observations had been previously recorded. The pattern of the moons Ganymede, Callisto, Io and its biggest moon Europa would give an indication of longitude by the times of their rising. All the ancients had to have, was a telescope, sandglass and some sort of tables that recorded the times of the moons rising based on Heliopolis for example. We must assume

that the people who fabricated this box did have
some sort of telescope otherwise why did they go to
so much trouble to give us the clues using the
pictures? They must have had knowledge and skills
beyond our belief.

Then knowing that the sunset changes, along with
the length of the day, recorded on some form of
sundial, they would have an approximate terrestrial
time. Using the sandglass they could then observe
the moons and read the difference in time with
respect to sunset. This would give a ball park figure
and at least assist in navigation.'

Khalid replied ' Yes Anna It was the ancient
Egyptians who divided the day into twenty-four
hours and they were also aware of precession of the
planets. After all their religion was in the worship
of the celestial god Ra and they knew that he
brought the seasons and the annual inundation.
They thus had plenty of time to study astronomy. It
is not so unbelievable when you look at the
pyramids and the fact that their sides lie exactly
along the cardinal axis North, South, east and West
that they could have worked out a method to
position things exactly on a specific point on the
surface of the earth. I still wonder how they
managed to do it. Even with the machines we have
today it would be a gigantic task'

I suggested we all call time as my will was fading like the day. 'Perhaps the answers we seek are not here but have been removed elsewhere.' We all agreed that tomorrow might be better and Anna sat beside me holding my now sweaty hand. ' You have suffered so much during the last few days Caro. I think it is about time that we use others to search for us. Gentlemen are there any other archives we might use to see if these things tie in with any specific period in history?'

'What do you mean Anna?' asked Khalid. 'I think that such a traumatic and terrible end to a king must have been written down for posterity by someone. Either as a contemporary or at some time shortly after. If what we experienced has any meaning, then it is based upon fact. . Someone might have recorded it. It cannot be possible that the only record of this king is a few boxes and a hawk statue. There must be something more.'

Imir who had been quiet until now suggested we looked in the archives of the Cairo museum as he was aware that there were some undeciphered papyrus scrolls that had been testing some of the scholars there for quite a time. 'Why do we not go there and continue our search? I shall arrange transport for early tomorrow morning, say three-o clock? We have a flight going north and can be on it. That will give you eight hours sleep at least my friends'

I looked around at everyone. ' Thanks Imir, that seems a good idea. I for one agree. It is about time we got to the truth and I would like to sort this thing out.'

We all said our goodnights and Anna remained beside my bed for a while. 'Francis, I am worried that all is not as it seems. There are too many things happening at once to understand. I would like to discover what our enemies are currently doing. I would like to have some idea who they actually are. I know that you are the prey. I do not know who are the hunters.'

'Darling I am sure that we will soon find out, in time I hope for us to do something about it. I am so tired that if I cannot get some sleep, I will not be able to go at all.'

Kissing me softly she smiled and left.

Chap 20

'El Qahira! The mother of the world.' Khalid said,
'Or Cairo as you know it. My family is here; I have
not seen them for a while. You must visit my house'
I looked at the obvious excitement in his face, and I
liked him more. He was a man who was proud of
his heritage and culture. He had saved my life and I
felt safe in his presence. ' Come and see the
Pyramids, look how magnificent they are'
Anna and I moved closer to the windows as the big
military aircraft banked slightly left and the great
monuments slid into sight.
We had not prepared ourselves for the visual
impact of an aerial view. The Sun peeking over the
eastern horizon on our right produced a golden
light, which cast giant triangular shadows
highlighting the geometric precision of this ancient
monument with incredible contrast. We gazed
down on the last remaining wonder of the world. I
could just make out the sphinx, crouched like a cat
at the foot of the man made mountains looking
forever out over the Nile. It was a moment to
treasure. ' I did not know they were so close to the
city' said Anna. 'Yes it is unfortunate that el Giza is
now just a suburb.' Khalid said sadly.
Cairo sprawled out in front of our aircraft like a
sinuous dun coloured maze rising out of the desert.

It seemed that had attached itself to the great Nile.
Its expanse reached all around us, the rising sun
was now extinguishing the twinkling streetlights
with the gold of dawn.

Our plane gently turned right and crossed the wide
river. Khalid our guide continued. 'See the citadel
of Salladin. It is very old. We looked upon the
massive crenellated walls that were embracing the
hill on which it stood. Minarets from numerous
mosques reached out as if to claw us from the sky
as we descended still further on what I took to be
our landing approach to the airport at Heliopolis,
the city of the sun.

We touched down gently and the plane came to a
halt alongside a nondescript building far from the
main terminal. A motorcycle escort was already
waiting for us, their uniforms well pressed and
extremely smart. It looked as though they had been
preparing for hours. They shot to attention as Imir
led us through the exit and down the stairs. A large
Russian built Zil with tinted windows and mirror
like paintwork swallowed the four of us like a
ravenous beast as the engine growled with the
strain of the air conditioning.

We left the airport with a wail of sirens as the early
commuting traffic was herded out of the way by
our outriders. I could not help but smile as an irate

camel refused the honking and cursing, blocking
the road enough to slow us down for a few seconds.
As we passed the Heliopolis Sheraton on our left,
Khalid pointed and exclaimed. 'This is your hotel,
we shall return here later if we have the time.' The
car plus the wailing motorcycles was now joining a
modern elevated freeway and climbed above the
roofs of the houses when Khalid continued. 'I shall
now explain this strange city as we enter. Cairo is
really two cities, the Metropolis or city of the living
over there on our right; and the Necropolis or city
of the dead on our left. You see. We Egyptians
believe in keeping our traditional tombs, even
though as Moslems we believe that it is the soul that
survives death. Our Muslim ancestors built their
moulids or cemeteries in the desert to the east, in
the direction of Mecca, and not in the west towards
the setting sun.'
We looked at what would appear to be a town with
houses and streets. There were mosques and street
signs. There were however, no telephone cables or
shops, just the occasional street light, A few people
were walking around, but there was none of the
frenetic activity to which we had grown
accustomed. To the uneducated eye, they were like
any other street, in any other town, except that the
houses were really family tombs where generations
of the cities dead had been laid to rest. 'Things are

changing. The population of the city is growing and
we now have people living here among the dead.
We call them tomb squatters. Can you imagine it?'
I looked at Khalid and simply nodded adding.
'After a week or so in this wonderful country,
Khalid, I can imagine just about anything.' We all
laughed at the obvious truth in my statement.
Our motorcade now came alongside the wonderful
citadel that caught the light of the new dawn. I saw
the round towers spaced regularly along the high
walls. They seemed to spring from the sedimentary
sandstone escarpment like giant trees. I thought
that this place had seen much intrigue and power
come and go. Looking up towards the western sky,
still bearing the traces of night made quite a
contrast because the ancient ramparts stood out in
burning iridescence, it was as though fire had
descended upon them. All too soon the moment
passed forever.
The car was slowing down and turned right up a
short hill against the flow of traffic, and entered this
subject of my thoughts through a well-guarded
gateway. Regardless of our obvious pedigree, we
were inspected prior to the barrier being lifted and
entry granted. Imir spoke to Khalid quietly, they
both nodded. He then turned to us and explained
'we have just entered el-Qal'a the citadel via the
desert gate. Apart from its position, this place holds

The National Police Museum and over there in the
el Harim Palace is the Military Museum. Of course
this area is most secure. It has to be, as you will
soon realise.

We left the cool interior of our car and I felt the
stirring warmth of the surrounding desert that
would lift the temperature towards its noontime
peak. The sun was illuminating the upper walls of
the courtyard and I could see the Muhammad Ali
Mosque with its enormous central dome that sat
upon four others catching the warming rays. Anna
was as spellbound as I was, with nature's
paintbrush of early morning sunlight that decorated
this sparse but interesting landscape.

'Come on both of you, we must not keep them
waiting' said Imir. We entered a very old wooden
doorway. The giant reinforcing studs, each as big as
a fist made it look a bit intimidating. I could not
help but notice the modern hinges and locking
system along with the cameras and concrete anti
ram bollards disguised as seating just inside the
entrance.

Climbing an exquisitely carved marble staircase,
and passing along a corridor hung with tapestries,
we were shown into a side room with polished
wood floor and a large table. Brass ornamental
objects were in its centre and they reflected the
sunlight into my eyes. I could make out two or

three men sitting with their faces turned towards us.

Both Khalid and Imir snapped to attention and saluted. Khalid caught hold of my right arm, and before I had time to gather my wits or vision again, he was propelling Anna and me towards these people. 'Mr President, may I introduce Mr Francis Edwards and Mrs Anna Scarletti'

We both looked into the tired face of Hosni Mubarak, President of Egypt. Coming round the table, he smiled and took both our hands in his. Two large men standing behind him, whom I took to be bodyguards, simply scowled at this break from protocol. 'Welcome to Cairo' he said in accented English. He smiled at us both, and I could see the alert expression in his eyes. I was sure they missed nothing. 'You definitely look like your picture, no wonder you caused quite a stir. I am sorry that your stay has been so unlucky. And this is your radiant lady, I am charmed to meet you too'

All I could say was how pleased I was to meet him and that he need not worry too much as I was now getting over my previous problems. Anna was going through the same word famine as myself. After all, I thought, it is not every day you meet a head of state, is it?

His security men were ever watchful, even in this room. They were being exceedingly careful. There

were many reasons to be cautious. He had
problems with militant Islamists. They saw him as
anti-Arab these militants had attacked and killed
dozens of foreign tourists. He had supported the
UN sanctions against Iraq and promoted close ties
with Israel. He had tried to broker peace between
the Palestinians and the Israelis on many occasions.
The home economy was in tatters with large
unemployment, which had fuelled discontent.
I had seen this man many times on the news. I had
always admired his stance for peace against all
odds. He had been elected soon after Sadat was
slain in October 1981. Had it been that long ago?
Here we were in the new millennium and he was
still fighting the warmongers. Now I was involved
and had to fight also.
I was unsure whether I was up to it. I was no James
Bond and certainly had little or no experience of
subterfuge on this level. My attempts so far had
been inhibited by my inability to realise the intrigue
and sub plots we had been submerged within. This
had nearly cost me my life on at least two occasions.
Now that I was on the mend I could hopefully
assist, to put an end to this mystery.
'Please be seated, you must be thirsty, I shall
organise refreshments.' He gently gave the orders
and miraculously the sweet tea arrived within

seconds. I used the short time to collect my wits as not to appear stupid or out of place.

Mubarak sat down facing us. He clasped both hands together and rested his chin upon them. Looking over my shoulder he spoke 'You will deliver your report Superintendent Khalid?' My friend solemnly nodded and rose to his feet. An officer stepped from behind me and handed him a large dossier tied with a green ribbon. Starting slowly he turned the pages and began to speak. 'Mr President, I might at some time have recourse to ask Mr Edwards certain questions to clarify my report. I have given him your word as instructed that he may answer without fear of any action being taken against him.' Drinking slowly I nodded my affirmation whilst Khalid recounted the last few days adventures augmenting them with excerpts from reports from both police and military sources. I was surprised at the detail, and how much trouble I had caused the police in the early stages of the enquiry by simply staying silent.

There had been rumours circulating for quite some time before my arrival in Egypt, of the existence of artefacts leading to the whereabouts of a new tomb being discovered. A Polaroid picture of a Pharaoh, unknown to Egyptologists was circulating the underworld. The rumours also told of a priceless treasure set of boxes that came with the picture.

Thus the stage had been set for my entrance into this web of intrigue and death.

A man who matched the photograph had been seen in Luxor. Khalid had been dispatched by presidential order to investigate the truth and to report. He had arrived in Luxor and learned about the Murders on the West Bank, both those of the workmen who had discovered the artefacts, and those of the two suited strangers I had seen die, at Medinet Habu.

He had discovered the whereabouts of the man in the photograph, namely myself. This man had subsequently had his hotel room burgled. He had been beaten but was not permanently hurt. I felt that I should disagree with that one as I still could feel the stitches in the back of my head, but I remained silent as Khalid continued his narrative.

It was then that Khalid was able to put Anna and I under surveillance. He had thus known of our visit to Jibril in hospital, and had also known of the others who were following us. They had been identified as contract killers. That was the reason he had been so close as to save my life

Upon discovering the magnitude of the case, he had requested help. Imir had thus also been brought in to assist Khalid, using the military facilities to give me extra protection and medical treatment subsequent to the second attempt on my life in a civilian hospital.

Khalid ran through the events leading up to our quasi séance when I discovered my alter ego.

' I am sure that you have seen the Video recording Mr President?'

Mubarak nodded to Khalid and replied 'There are many unexplained things throughout our history, but the sheer number of coincidences in this matter defy logic or reason. I am inclined to believe what I saw. There is a power from beyond our comprehension at work here'

At this point Khalid brought out the boxes for the president to examine. Being this close to a world leader, I noted the intensity of the man. He was older than I had realised and extremely intense and focussed. He turned each item over and over for what seemed an eternity before passing comment.

'What do you think Francis?' he said.

'I am not quite sure Mr President, I know that there is some mystical power that was triggered when these items came into my life. I have become an ancient pharaoh and find I understand things of which I have no experience.' He looked me straight in the eye and simply said, 'I believe you.'

I saw the sense in this discourse concerning my alter ego and realised that I was not dreaming any of it.

Even a president believed me.

'We have a picture of an ancient Pharaoh who looks exactly like this man,' Khalid said touching me on the shoulder. 'We have the attention of at least three secret service agencies, two of whom known to be hostile to him and to Egypt. We have treasure of great value; he alone can locate.' Pointing to us in turn with his giant hands and then to himself, he continued.

'The result of my investigations has been based upon my experiences also. It has been necessary for us to come to Cairo to see if we can shed further light on the facts concerning the circumstances leading to the death of this pharaoh who was called Geb. At least we have a name. Francis has deciphered the disks. As you will have noticed, they are more of a warning than a story.

One thing is very clear. We four have some ancient bond that ties us together, but which we still cannot fathom. There are others outside who also are tied through this bond, one of who is the assassin named Ali who I arrested whilst Francis was in the first hospital.'

I remembered the event with some humour. Looking at Anna, it was obvious that she did too. Although the man had been there to kill me, the sheer power of Khalid was amazing. It was a miracle that the unsuccessful assassins' neck was not broken.

Khalid nodded to one of his men who left the room. Seconds later he was back with the man who had tried to kill me. Our eyes met. Did I know this person? I looked at the restraining chains that tied his hands to his body. He looked from me to Mubarak, then back again and fell to his knees, gibbering.' I offer you profuse apologies. I had no desire to offend you my pharaoh. If I had known my actions were against you, I would never have tried to hurt you. I did not know it was you. The people who told me to do it said it was to save you.' He wept . 'Great and immortal Geb please forgive me.'

Our eyes met as he squirmed and a cold realisation washed over me. I had known him well

Chap 21

I recognised this man; he belonged in my past.
Perhaps he was telling the truth, I stood up and
proceeded to become Geb for a few moments. 'Look
at me.' I said in that language I thought only I
understood. His face went white, which for an Arab
I thought is quite difficult. He cried out in a loud
voice 'Agha umad!' which I was subsequently
informed means the master has returned, then he
prostrated himself, his outstretched form face down
on the wood floor; his arms still bound, squirming
in his discomfort. 'Hail Geb Father of all gods and
patriarch of Egypt and her kings, I seek your
forgiveness for my sins. I am as the desert dust in
your presence and would die a million deaths
rather than harm your sanctified person. Do you
not remember your humble slave Bushir?'
'Get up I said in English, you will not be harmed if
you are open and honest with us.'
I held his gaze, he was more afraid of me than his
president. Perhaps he would help us to unravel this
mystery. 'Who told you to kill me? I command you
to tell us everything.'
'Shukran sayidi thank you sir' He spluttered, his
shaking growing less pronounced.
He proceeded to empty his very soul, his eyes never
leaving my face. We learned of a tall dark haired
man, an Iraqi named Malik, who two months before

had brought a large number of men into his village and intimidated many of its inhabitants.

Malik was also in collusion with many local policemen and politicians who consolidated his position by simply ignoring any complaints. Ali, formally Bushir had been drawn into this conspiracy by a feeling that he really did belong. 'I felt that I knew this man from long ago. I felt we were like brothers. He was kind to me in my former life.'

I stopped him here to ask him the names of those in charge that had let this evil go unchallenged. He recounted name after name and I noted that Khalid's man was scribbling furiously. 'Why do you think he needed so many people?' I asked. ' We were all looking for something. Every day groups would go out into the desert and use machines to see below the sand. He used the balloon to examine the cliffs and wadis. We were told where to look but I am sure that nothing was found.'

I secretly prayed that he was right. What motive did Malik have? Who were his backers? How was he so well connected?

'He is possibly, as far as we can find out from Mossad, a member of Sadam Hussein's secret police or possibly a member of Amn-al-Khass Sadam Hussein's personal Presidential Security Force among other things but nobody knows anything about him. All we have to go on is rumour and conjecture. We have no photograph or better description. Some have even said he is European or American' Khalid explained.

Ali continued his narrative of intimidation, fear and torture. More facts and places were mentioned but I felt that this was not leading us nearer the truth we sought.

I excused him and requested that he be removed and well treated. This having been done I collected my thoughts and tried to reason why and what exactly they had been looking for. They had at least six weeks start on us. What clues and what information did they have? And who was this Iraqi? By his description I had a vague recollection that perhaps I knew him too. Was he part of my past also?

'Francis you obviously do not see the significance of this mans name Malik? It means King or master. I supposed that you might know who it is we might be dealing with now?'

Imir now took the floor describing talks he had with the Israeli secret agency Mossad and the CIA they had informed him of an attempt by extremists to obtain either weapons-grade Plutonium from the Russian Mafia. Either that or an atom bomb. The asking price was fifty million dollars. They needed to find a lot of treasure to pay for it.

'El Salil ul Islam the sword of Islam' He said with resignation. 'What do you mean? I asked.

'Francis, whoever has this weapon, does not even have to use it. The fact that it can be placed anywhere gives our enemies the power to control the Arab world, or the rest of it for that matter. Just to threaten to place it here, in Cairo or Jerusalem, Jeddah or Tel Aviv would cause such panic and disruption that governments could not control. The extremists would tip the balance of power. No politician could risk the death of millions of innocent people by refusing to comply with their demands. We all know of course that they would actually detonate it without compunction or conscience. The stakes are enormous and go beyond comprehension'

'Why do they need the treasure Imir? Surely fanatics like Gadaffi or Sadam Hussein would finance the deal?' I asked.

'Look at it logically. If they were to finance such a weapon, the terrorists could even use it against them at some stage. Tripoli or Baghdad, they don't care. Also the rest of the world would punish any country that did broker such a terrible deal. These are evil men who do not care for the rights of anyone that opposes them. Remember they believe they are carrying out the will of Allah.'

' I suppose it could be stopped in Russia, surely the Russians do not want tactical warheads going missing? Or am I still being naïve?' I asked.

'The Russians have lost enough Plutonium to build at least twenty bombs. This would allow many parties to have a nuclear capability. I can assure you Francis; no country wants to make atomic weapons available, especially to terrorists. A lot of our intelligence comes from the Russian military. Do not forget that they were our allies once. As for building a bomb, there are many unemployed Russian nuclear scientists who can be bought for a few thousand dollars. It is all down to you now Francis to stop this horror. They must not find the treasure.'

I had to agree that it was not looking good. That left me in the front line. If I were alive, then whoever they were, believed I could lead them to the tomb, but someone wanted to kill me.

It was a contradiction of intent. It looked as though one faction thought I would be better dead than lead the other to the tomb and the other needed me alive. So who was the enemy?

Who actually wanted me alive? Could I call them enemies?

If I was the key, then who needed me alive? And who needed me dead? Malik wanted me dead but why? Surely I was of more use to him alive? He

after all, knew who I really was long before I did. It looked as though he wanted to find the tomb; he had been searching for something for weeks. Or perhaps now I was the competition? Outlining my thoughts to the group, I asked them if there was a possible explanation for attempts to kill me.
'I feel that some countries would rather you were dead than they become threatened' Said Anna. ' If you apply logic rather than sentiment, there are several candidates. Israel for example and certainly the CIA would not want the power base in the Middle East to change. Possibly the Russians too'
Mubarak nodded and said ' that is true, but we need to unravel the secrets you all share. It is not even required that the terrorists find the tomb. All that is needed is the rumour that they have the funds to carry out their plans. This would provide a reason for a Jihad or holy war. It provides a rallying point for all malcontents and enemies of my country. We must show the world that it is Egypt who owns her treasures and not terrorism. Francis, it is Egypt that will fall first. We must not fail'
I must confess that this made chilling sense. We had to visit the Cairo Museum of Antiquities to see if the truth lay there. This had been the reason I had wanted to come here; perhaps I would be able to decipher some of the papyrus scrolls that seemed to be written in my ancient script?

'How much time do we have?' I asked.

Mubarak stood and came round to me. His eyes were sincere and showed the burden he carried. 'There is so little time left. You shall have all the support you need. Do not fail, or peace will die. I shall make all things available to you. Just ask for what you want.'

He certainly convinced me that I could do something positive. even though I was slightly undecided and doubtful two minutes ago.

The thought that I could influence international politics was still out of my league; but if a President and half a dozen killers believed it too, then there must be some truth in it. The CIA and MOSSAD plus the Russians could be involved but if it all came down to me, then I could use all the help I could get.

Mubarak placed his hand on my shoulder and caught my eye. He spoke earnestly ' Francis it is most important that you may find what you seek. I must go now but please waste no time. The future seems to be in your hands and our past will be at your disposal.'

He shook my hand and left amongst a cordon of bodyguards and personal staff. My companions visibly relaxed and the tension diminished a little. We all discussed the implications of the facts now shared by all of us.

There had to be some form of conspiracy that went to the highest level, and on a worldwide scale. Who was behind it and what did they hope to gain? I felt the answers might be found in the Cairo Museum and requested that we go on down and see what facts awaited locked in the enigmatic writings that had withstood those who had sought them.

Chap 22

What can one say, when everything that has been normal unto now, has become a pale imitation of normality? My perception of myself had been that of a man reaching his middle age. I had at one time wanted to be a grandfather and to enjoy the warmth of an extended family life. There were things that had been important to me in my youth that were now insignificant and useless. I now had the duality of two lifetimes to contend with. It was as though I had found an understanding companion. Not bad, but this companion was within my very self. My values were tainted by the responsibilities I had obviously and unwillingly inherited along with the boxes.

The vague recollection of a previous life was just below my conscious thoughts. I wondered if my feelings were unique. They were to me at this moment. I had become two independent personalities at the same time. It made me aware that as a race of beings, mankind had not changed much over the last five thousand years at least.

As I looked around the museum with its collections of artefacts, each made with loving care and an attention to detail; I felt an understanding of the full reasons for their existence. They were no longer just curios, they were living messages, and they were talking to my soul.

As we walked between the various statues and objects, I was aware of the tension that these things evoked within me. I had no idea why this should be so, but it was real, and detracted from my excitement from being in a place I had always dreamed of visiting. This was the very epicentre of ancient Egyptian history for me. Other museums may have exhibits of great importance but this was the only grand museum in Egypt. I had the best opportunity to enjoy this moment but I did not feel like a visitor, I felt like an exhibit. I silently told myself not to be so stupid and I held Anna's hand as she seemed to enjoy the multitude of statues and objects.

'Here we are' said Imir. 'This is Sawsan, she will show you what you seek'

I looked at the small, dark haired pretty woman who stood in the doorway; she smiled and came forward.

'I am pleased to meet you,' I said noticing her absolute enthusiasm for knowledge, she trembled slightly as we shook hands; like an anxious child who cannot wait to start.

'Let me assure you Mr. Edwards, it is I who am most pleased to meet you. The moment I first heard of your abilities, I have waited impatiently for this

moment. In this room are many scrolls that have
never been deciphered. I have been informed you
may be able to read some of the hieroglyphs, they
do not follow the normal pattern and phonetic
form. We hope you will provide us with the means
to understand them. I have chosen those with
writing that matches the symbols on the boxes'
Turning, she led us into a well-lit room hung with
tapestries and having a long wooden table with
matching chairs and individual green shaded
reading lamps.

There were long scrolls, set under glass, lined up
along the entire expanse of the polished surface.
The papyrus was very aged, and bits were missing
in places, but the script looked familiar to me. I
looked at a long strip that was covered in pictures.
It reminded me of the Bayeux Tapestry which
portrays the Norman Invasion. I mentioned this,
and Sawsan took a microphone and clipped it onto
my collar. 'Please speak into this Mr. Edwards,
would you read the writing out loud first, and then
provide us with an approximate translation' I
nodded, my eyes drawn to what might be the
answer to all that had happened in the last ten days.
It seemed more than that but I had lived a few
lifetimes since then.

The others stood around me as I looked at the
writings of a man who had been dead for thousands

of years. Everyone was silent as I mouthed the text. The microphone picked up the pronunciation of a language unknown to all but a few. I first had to read the story and then to try and translate its meaning.

It told of a man who had come from the stars. He taught peace and understanding and showed kindness to all.

He had built a palace and had married a beautiful Queen. They had shown how to harness the bounty of the Nile. He had used the natural stone to build wonderful things and had demonstrated the power of science. There was prosperity and a rule of enlightenment. Artists had developed and spread the wonder of creativity.

His name was Geb and it was said that he had lived for many lifetimes. He had many sons who it was hoped, would continue the progress and consolidate the kingdom. Then one day Geb was dead and many of his sons too. He was buried in a tomb that he had constructed, prior to his death. Not soon after the period of mourning he had decreed, had elapsed, a civil war broke out, and the last of his sons, his favourite general and the head of his household were killed. His Prime minister had taken over and the once prosperous country had declined within a few years.

Outsiders had invaded and taken the beautiful
objects and those able to make them, away to other
lands. It had been many years before beauty
returned to Egypt. The writer had not given too
much detail but had covered the basic facts of a
dynasty that had fallen through the ambition of a
usurper who had not been able to continue to
sustain the kingdom he had stolen. It was more a
lament than a chronology, more a lesson of greed
and power being the root of evil. Whilst it did not
give specific names and dates, it was obviously
meant to be a general newspaper of the time.
I heard the words I spoke reverberate around the
room. It was not exactly my voice, but nothing
surprised me anymore. I indicated that I had
finished reading the large scroll and Sawsan placed
another in front of me. This one showed the
judgement of Thoth and was annotated in the same
script and language I had just translated. It looked
similar to the box lid that I had first seen in Jibril's
house, but more worn by time. There was extra
writing around the edges. I asked for a magnifying
glass and was able to see the four moons of Jupiter
clearly defined.
It was directed at me 'Oh Geb you are reborn. Only
you can read this. Your enemy now returns from
Babylon and brings the wrath of his king to destroy
your chosen country. Remember the plains of

Thebes and the sacred mountain. Look to the West
and the setting sun and the land of Nut, Queen of
the night, and you will find the place you seek. Use
the eye of Horus to mark the gateway of your Ka
and the path to heaven. I Yussef, priest of Isis,
placed your Ba in the sacred ground to return when
the sands of time are almost spent. I left with you
the power you now seek. I pray your heart is no
heavier than the feather of truth and that your Ka
walks with the gods. Let you live forever and return
to this your land, when many read your name. I
thus pray you will read this message one-day.
There shall be many copies of this pledge placed
throughout the kingdom so that the years will not
erase the wonder of your being. May Ra carry you
on his journey across the sky for all time '
Another scroll told of the treachery behind the
death of a gentle king. His Prime Minister had
allegedly poisoned him by scratching him,
apparently by accident, with a sharp stick possibly
covered in snake venom. The death had been fairly
quick. I knew at this moment that it had not been
so. I had been alive for a long time, paralysed, and
unable to move or cry out, unable to lift a finger to
say I could see and hear. I knew that it had been the
poison from a Mamba. That snake paralyses the
victim and gives the impression of death. I recalled

my funeral experience in the Luxor hospital as the impact of the truth hit me like a solid rock.

Until this moment I understood that I had not truly believed that I was really the dual person, other than by accident. I suppose I had thought that a force from outside myself possessed me. That was not true, I was Geb reincarnated! The finding of the box had started the saga.

Another who was also like me, aware that he was reincarnated had said my true name. I tried to remember his; I could see his eyes filled with hate. He had killed me. As much as I tried, I was unable to speak it. A deep fear made me avoid even thinking it. I must not dwell upon his name. I felt hate at the thought of his existence and the treachery I had suffered.

I knew why the name of this murderer was not written. It was so his Ka could not draw strength from the immortality of a name. My children had been slain by this man. He had usurped my kingdom and destroyed all that I had tried to create. Worse still, I had trusted and loved him as a friend and had treated him as part of my family.

My queen had been banished, far away to the east and had died there soon after. My faithful priest Yussef had vanished and my tomb had been violated. If that was so, then what did Yussef mean in his narrative and message directed to me? I felt tears cascade down my cheeks as I remembered the happiness I had felt in the company of one I had loved so much, playing with our sons. I mourned the fact they had been left for the jackals and beasts of the desert to devour.

Anna stood behind me and hugged me to her. Nestling her face beside mine she softly said, 'Caro, dearest, I feel your pain but I do not understand what it actually means. I know that I am involved somehow, but I do not understand why I feel so sad. I love you and wish to help'

Looking to my right I saw tears in the eyes of all-present as they too shared my grief. It had taken me thousands of years to mourn the souls of my family. I also knew that those around me had been involved in my life before. Imir had been my general, Khalid had run my household and Anna had been my wife. I also knew that they too were beginning to realise the parts they had played so many years ago. I now needed to know the present day name of the person who had been my Prime Minister. I did not want to believe what I was thinking but the power of the revelation was too much to endure.

'Is it fate that rules our lives? Or do we rule our fate?' said Khalid. 'What do you think we can do to stop this person finding what we all seek?' he continued.

We all started talking as the bubble of grief burst with the realisation and indignation of our common past and common enemy.

All that remained now was to seek out the man who wanted to destroy the country we loved. Thanking Sawsan who assured me that I had unravelled a new path in Egyptology. I left the room; my resolve set on revenge. I had to decipher the message Yussef had written in his prophecy. He had reburied my Ba or body in a sacred place that we once knew. He had set the clues up for me should I not remember. I needed to get back to Luxor and the West Bank to seek the final truth but first there were things I had to do.

We crossed the great frenetic square to the Mugamma government building that housed a multitude of civil service departments. It had been a Russian inspired concrete tower that was totally out of keeping with the rest of the area around the square. I watched the preparations outside the Umar Makram Mosque for what Khalid told me were for a funeral. Great tents were being erected and lined with beautiful carpets for the guests. Anna and I held hands and watched as a worker who was at least twenty feet up a ladder walked it by rocking it from side to side like a circus performer along the garlands and fairy lights he was attaching to the street lamp posts. His balance

was remarkable as he avoided the many
pedestrians about their business in the square.
With Khalid in front, we entered the foyer and I
was aware of the dilapidation, there was no fancy
welcoming decoration. Everything was functional
and utilitarian. 'This is the local office, I have to
make a few arrangements before we return. I have
also set up a meal, as you must surely be hungry.
We will eat first then I will sort those matters, it will
only take a few minutes'
'Khalid, is there a fishing tackle shop in this great
city of yours? Or do I have to scour the markets for
some items I require?' I said watching the
astonishment in his face. He rolled his great hands
with his fingers pointing upwards. 'Francis, where
we are going, there is no water even to drink! There
are however great fish to be caught in Lake Nasser.
I have been informed that some of them can eat a
man but as we are not even within five hundred
miles of there, I sometimes wonder if your recent
adventures have damaged your logic. Yes, we have
all things available in most places providing you
know where to look. What do you want fishing
rods for anyway?'
Not wanting to disturb my train of thought, I
simply told him I did not need a rod and reel and
that I would give him further details later. I had
expected him to be more demanding but he simply

winked conspiratorially at me, his warm brown
eyes reassuringly smiling.

We were then shown into a canteen that obviously
was for management. A small meal was served and
our group sat silently now, each of us knowing that
the next few hours would be crucial for our
survival. It was almost like the Last Supper because,
even whilst among my friends I could not push
away the hidden messages of Yussef about betrayal.
Who was he trying to warn me about? First the
golden disks and now the papyrus I had just read in
the museum.

A plain-clothes policeman whom I recognised from
having seen him at the Joliville Hotel in Luxor
arrived with a cardboard box. Khalid spoke to him
and the man went out. Khalid then turned to me
and winked. He was truly acting strangely. I
nudged him in an attempt to find out what was
going on and he indicated we leave the room.

'I have a surprise for Francis, I am sure he will show
you all later but now it is just we two who have to
talk.' We left the others, now slightly inquisitive by
our behaviour, and entered another office where the
box had been taken. It sat upon a metal-framed
table illuminated by a single bare bulb. Khalid
opened the top flap, his large form casting a stark
shadow into the interior so that I could not see what
it contained. 'I hope this is what you require

Francis, I assumed that since you are not intending
to fish then all that remains are hook and line. I
have no idea why you require either but I took the
opportunity to procure some for you.' He handed
me a packet of fishhooks and two large reels of
fishing line. 'Thanks friend, you are a good
detective.' I said 'Why did you not give me these in
front of the others?'

Khalid replied, looking me directly in the eyes; his
voice was charged with emotion. 'You suspect a
traitor in our midst and so do I. Things have been
hidden from us for too long. Remember that I
personally interrogated the man you saw today and
have known of the existence of the enemy for a
week now. I have been faced with a wall of silence
from every side both civilian and military. No
person seemed to have heard of this Malik until you
came into our country but he has been active in
Luxor for months in his search for whatever is out
there. You must understand that we police have
had several seemingly unconnected events on the
west bank, which until last week were but singular
cases of missing persons and the usual murder or
two. When I investigated you after the break-in at
your hotel and that gunfight at Medinet Habu I was
frustrated by your apparent innocence especially as
you had suffered an attack. I felt something for you
then, and of course time has proven the bond

between us. Unfortunately the answer to betrayal is hidden in history. We are going to have to find the truth and only you can lead us to it. The enemy also is aware that you are the only one who can trace the past so they have planted someone within our forces. I know this because they have until now remained undetected. How would they have known who you were in the first instance if they had no spy inside the police force or military? Who could let them know where you were staying or even your name? Somebody on high had pulled the strings. This was bigger than Egypt itself. The organisation and its ability to operate without problems must be due to external control. I recalled the satellite telephones and the obvious technical support plus the funds I had purloined. I had taken at least one hundred thousand dollars from my would-be killers at Medinet Habu.

Who had sent the second pair to rob me? Was it the same person who had sent the first? Interesting that because they would have had to have known or suspected that I acutely had the objects. As for the third pair on the motorbike; they would have had to know exactly where I was at a specific time. The fourth attempt had been a single individual specifically set to get me inside a secure hospital. Whoever was in control certainly had a lot of clout. It was enough to drive me paranoid.

I still could not understand who wanted me dead and who wished me to live.

Know your enemy. My own words stung me. I had not known my enemy was so close to me. What did I really know about Imir? I knew that he was ruthless and daring. He had operated in full view of the authorities without hindrance for a long time. How was he able to do that? I began to hypothesise the ways he could have operated. Corruption? Money? Fear? Hadn't Jibril said that a workman labouring near here had found the relics? Was this part true? Did that make Jibril my enemy? Had I been given the boxes to find out what they could not? No, I reasoned because the exposure of the picture put him and any of his cronies in more danger. It had been the picture that had alerted the whole pack. So rule him out.

What then of Khalid? He had known I was in danger and had put himself in front of Anna and me to save our lives. He had to be a true friend. Now, when it came to Imir. I now had some serious doubts. At first he was so attentive and helpful but that would have been to his advantage. He could observe and learn my progress with little effort. He also had power and anonymity; this gave him information and control. He had connections up to the president himself. He was beyond suspicion, or was he? Did the disks warn me about him? If so, then how could the writer know what might happen unless this was some form of bizarre game to be played out through eternity? I could almost feel myself laughing within my soul at the irony of it but Anna liked him. Why? Was there something from our combined past that I had overlooked? Unfortunately for me I was at a disadvantage because when you are normal a crisis like this is all that you have to concentrate on. I had two points of view within one soul, mine! I really had to let my real instinct control me and not allow my intellect to reign. How could I let it happen at all? Was there a magic means to let Geb loose? I really hoped there was. But what if it was none of these people? Yussef kept on telling me that he was with me always. Did he mean me? Could I be my own enemy having more than one persona?

'I think you have some explaining to do Khalid my friend'

'I know Francis but you will have to be patient a little while longer' 'Why? I am so confused by all of this. Don't I have enough to contend with by becoming more than one person?'

'That is the problem Francis you might be even more than that. It is possible to unhinge this country at this moment. There is much instability and unrest all around the Middle East. What concerns me is that others might be trying to

manipulate you. At one time you may have been a
King, I am trying to make sure you do not become a
pawn as so many others have in the past.'
'What sort of hold could they have over me? Or
anyone else for that matter?'
'You would be surprised. Remember that I am also
involved as much as you are. I have known who
you are for a long time, longer than you have. I
mean as long as those boxes were out of the ground.
I have my spies also. There has been much activity
prior to your visit to Egypt. Your arrival has served
to be the catalyst that has started the final reaction.'
'Khalid, I know you to be a friend and faithful
companion. You have saved my life at risk to your
own. I trust you, so why do you not fully trust me?'
'It is simple. I believe your ability to read the secret
writing might not be entirely unique. There may be
others also who can make sense of it. To put it
simply I feel that you are burdened with enough
worries and problems and would not act naturally.
All this is new to you but others have waited many
years for your arrival. This I am sure of.'
'Well fate may have drawn me here but it certainly
has drawn everyone else too. Do you think that a
greater power than us is in control then? I know
that I do'
'That may be so. It is possible that we are all players
or parts of a great plan but it seems beyond my

comprehension for now. All I know is that we are in danger and we should be very careful whom we trust. From the devices you took off the fatalities at Medinet Habu, and their passports I was convinced a foreign power possibly Israel or her ally America were behind their activities and also the fact that they spoke in English indicates that possibly they were not working for Malik. The satellite phone is untraceable and thus it could belong to anyone. Despite my inquiries, I have not found where it is registered because it has been turned off remotely. Possibly it is a CIA plaything. The Global Position System is of military quality and can therefore give the highest accuracy.'

'I am not surprised Khalid, it seems the rest of the world does not want a rogue bomb out there either. Why would the CIA want to have a go at me? It may have been them who just wanted to find the tomb first and thus stop whoever this Malik person is from getting it. I suppose that Mossad would be playing the same game too.'

I looked at him quizzically, he said nothing but simply nodded with a resignation that betrayed his own fatigue. I realised that this man had been hyperactive whilst I slept. He had been protecting me all along and just wanted to get this thing over with, as did I. 'Come on Khalid let us get back to our meal, as I am truly hungry and I get the

impression that we will not get too many more
chances to eat until this matter is over.'
The big man looked straight at me with his
knowing expression and warm brown eyes. I knew
we were like brothers at that moment. 'How much
do you really know my friend?' I asked.
'Sufficient to realise that we will change history if
we fail, we have little time to lose now and so we
must return to Luxor without further delay. How
do you feel about that?'
I did not answer because I was halfway through the
door.

Chap 23

The Hercules bumped along the taxiway. Sand
stirred by the prop-wash tumbled behind and
formed patterns on the tarmac. The soldiers
accompanying us settled into the bucket seats
amongst the cargo netting adorning the aircraft
walls. The interior of this cavernous vehicle was
well worn and functional and we too settled down
into the hammock-like webbing seats. We were up
front out of the slipstream behind the sand-
coloured vehicles that were attached by great straps
to large buckle-like clamps fixed to the metal floor. I
felt that it was like being in an old bus that rattled,
roared and groaned at every turn. All this I thought
and we were still on the ground! It was too loud to
talk, so we just sat there watching the runway
rushing into the distance past the open loading bay
door. Our shadow, running alongside seemed to be
a gigantic vulture in pursuit as it made its way over
the contours of the sand. The engines increased
revolutions as we slowly rose into the Cairo haze
and the sunlight entered our open door and darted
across while the aircraft turned south. Then it
became darker and the resonance of the airframe
tingled itself into my tired body like a relaxing
massage. Before I knew it I had drifted into the land
of Morpheus beyond all physical care.

Anna woke me in her usual loving gentle manner
and yet again I looked into those wonderful eyes. I
smiled and sat upright; no mean feat in a webbing
seat. 'Caro I'm sorry to break into your dreams but I
felt you would want to see this,' She said.

I looked out of the open cargo door to see the Nile
and the temples of Karnak spread beneath like a
giant metropolis painted carpet in the afternoon
heat. Shadows stood like solid black holes in the
dusty ground. The upturned faces of the many ant-
sized tourists looking at our aircraft, flying
overhead contrasted with the sheer size of the
pillars and columns and put the monument into
perspective; for without a measure of scale I would
not have believed how massive it truly was. We
passed over the outskirts of Luxor and made our
approach to the airfield that served it.

The landing was noisy and interesting due to
having to observe it facing backward for the first
time in my life. The roar of the engines decreased
and the reverse thrust from the propellers brought
us to a sedate taxiing speed within a very short
time.

The soldiers were unhooking the vehicles as we
taxied and had the engines started ready to drive
down the ramp as we came to a halt. I noticed the
heat as the airflow diminished and prepared to exit
along with Anna. A klaxon sounded and the whine

of hydraulic motors preceded the dropping of the
loading ramp. We climbed aboard a big Toyota
Land-cruiser and were driven off the Hercules, our
driver smiling as he engaged the air conditioning.
Khalid and the General were in the larger
communications vehicle in front of us. Another
large transport vehicle drew up behind and our
escort squad climbed aboard. We waited until this
had been completed and the convoy made its way
to a gate guarded by a sandbagged outpost
amongst the palm trees; low, squat and menacing. It
was flanked by red and white painted forty-gallon
oil drums forcing us to weave towards it like a
driving skill test track. The long snout of the heavy
calibre machine gun pointed towards us
throughout. The soldiers there, seeing the superior
rank of the general went into express mode. The
guard turned out and a flustered officer then lifted
the gigantic red barrier to let us pass with the
minimum of delay, saluting as we drove by onto a
dusty road that skirted the city of Luxor.
It certainly looked as though we did not want the
jungle telegraph to warn those we sought on the
West Bank. I did believe however that the transport
plane that brought us here might have given the
game away so I asked the driver who reassured me
that this was the supply plane that normally flew in
today.

We drove southwest with the sun streaming into
our eyes occasionally but the light really
accentuated the myriad plants, trees and birds. We
saw many Ibis, their long beaks curving, just like in
the papyrus pictures. The occasional Kingfisher,
startled by our passing would spread its
multicoloured wings and the metallic greens and
reds were wonderful to see. I had never seen
butterflies as big as birds before but what had
looked like flowers on a bush suddenly rose and
fluttered into the air scattering all around our
vehicle as we drove slowly by. Anna laughed like
an excited child at the beauty and novelty of these
giant flying works of art.
It was also interesting to see the irrigation channels
that spread out all over the place and the simple
road bridges that spanned them. I noticed that the
levels were controlled by numerous wheel-operated
sluice gates with the occasional shaduf to lift the
water for the large numbers of oxen and camels.
The vivid colours of the flora and the clothes of the
labourers tending the crops reminded me of the
eternal unchanging beauty of this land. Because we
had to follow the canals to the next bridge we were
being treated to an interesting tour of rural life. This
made for a pretty but indirect drive to the Nile
Bridge but the only traffic we encountered was a

few overloaded donkeys carrying sugar cane and a
motorcycle or two.

As we crossed the new bridge we could see the
Joliville, once our hotel, along on our right about
half a kilometre away on the banks of the river. I
remembered our having listened to La Boheme
there and the love I had found. The clock had run
on and taken us with its irreversible outpouring
current of time past. Feelings of I wish this had
never happened passed through me. As I
involuntarily gently squeezed her hand Anna
repeated what I had been thinking out loud and
added how much had passed in just a few days. We
both watched a little boat with two fishermen one
rowing, the other casting his net into the river
flowing beneath the concrete piers of the bridge;
this really was a land of contrast. No more words
were required, just our mutual love mixed with our
fear and the apprehension of what we were about
to encounter.

I kept on thinking about this mysterious man who I
felt I knew and feared. Yet my emotions seemed to
be on the periphery of my senses as though I was
watching a horror film and knew in the back of my
mind, that it was not real and whilst I could be
shocked, it would end soon. My conscious logic
however and the dull ache of the bullet wound told

me that the chances of a good ending were remote to say the least.

We drove into a military compound that obviously was there to defend the western side of the bridge. I saw the camouflage netting covering the gun and missile emplacements amongst the tall papyrus plants beside the Nile. There were large poorly constructed block built walls with Arabic numerals upon them and an Egyptian flag hung limply in the still air of the afternoon. The dust stirred by our entrance hung for what seemed an eternity before descending on the sentries who rushed to attend to the lead vehicle containing their General. Our Toyota went round a corner behind a wall and we were asked to wait, the driver opened his door onto the exceptional heat, which forced its way in before we realised how oven like it was. He left us but kept the engine and air conditioning running to minimise our discomfort.

'I had forgotten how hot it was away from the pool,' said Anna. 'The locals do not seem to mind however' I replied. We sat and watched the events outside and were pleased to see Khalid coming towards us. He motioned us to stay where we were and soon joined us along with another hot blast as the door was opened.

Settling himself into the passenger seat, he turned and wiping his brow said 'We are trying to keep

you out of sight for as long as possible but my men and the army have been out this morning seeking the terrorists. They have found only cheap crooks and malcontents as it seems the man and his companions have left in the last twenty-four hours. I am afraid we have no idea where they went or who they were. I am sure they have friends on high who have warned them of our coming but I am afraid that we are still unsure if they have achieved their purpose and that we may already be too late.'
'Where does that leave us?' said Anna 'What if they have found it and taken the gold? Are we too late?' She looked decidedly upset and I put my arms around her to assure her that we would be all right. 'Please don't get upset' I pleaded, 'I know that they have not found it because of what Yussef had written. Can't you see that our presence here has shaken them because they thought I was dead? You forget that they think I really know where it is. Anyway I would not be surprised if they try something soon to get at me again when we go hunting ourselves.'
I continued, directing my attention towards Khalid ' How long before we can try out the eye of Horus? It will be sundown in two hours or so and I would like to get cracking today.' He sat silent for a few moments considering my request and his eyes met mine 'Go then Francis, we shall organise a patrol

but if there is any danger, we must get you back to safety as you are the only solution to this problem. We cannot afford to lose your ability as I feel it will be up to you and you alone to end this matter.'

Chap 24

Half an hour later thirty or so men were accompanying us towards Medinet Habu. I sat in the front looking through the fragmented lens, trying to line up the various bits and to get an idea of our starting point in preparation for the appointed time. One image was constantly of the road about ten metres in front of the vehicle and no matter how I tried, I could not seem to line up the horizon or anything above it so that the image was further than that. What did it mean? If I were to lock one image of the setting sun and another of that pyramid shaped rock as I was trying now I was looking about 10 metres in front and if I kept on doing this I could make course corrections as the sun set. We were going almost due west now towards the edge of the escarpment the sun still had an hour or so left before it would descend below the hills. We had to be on the plain as Yussef directed and able to see the sunset but Yussef had said, ' look to the west and the setting sun.'

'Has anyone got a compass?' I shouted suddenly; my companions jumped at my return from my silent contemplation. 'Here Francis said Khalid, you will have to get outside away from the metal of the vehicle. We do have Global Positioning Systems in the truck if you want.'

'I asked the driver to stop and leaped out of the door in my enthusiasm. The air was noticeably cooler now as I stumbled away from the Toyota. The other vehicles fore and aft of us stopped and Imir set up a perimeter ordering his men into position as he walked towards me. 'What is it Francis? Have you found something?'

'I am not sure, ' I said but I think your pistol is affecting the compass. If you would be so kind to step back, I think I have an idea.' As Anna had said the Sun actually set in the Southwest because of our latitude but west was west and the ancients knew exactly where it was. I turned myself so that my right shoulder faced north and was thus looking west 'What is over there?' I asked pointing to the Northwest. Khalid replied 'That is the road to the valley of the Queens'

I jumped up and down in my excitement 'can't you see it was here all the time. The best place to hide a King was with the Queens especially the Queen of the night. Who would think of looking there amongst the hundreds of minor tombs for a King?'

'Mad but logical enough to mislead us all' Said Anna who was caught up in my enthusiasm. 'Let us make haste' said Imir making his way back to the lead vehicle. He shouted orders to his men and they speedily made their way back to the convoy. Anna, Khalid and myself got aboard our Toyota and

followed Imir up the incline towards the valley of
the Queens.
'All we have to do now is to find the eye of Horus
as described,' I said thoughtfully.
'Surely you have it' Khalid said. I did not quite
agree with him at this point. I had a niggling
suspicion that the words were more than just
superficial but were also concealed in paraphrase
and thus contained an encrypted message that used
our assumption rather than the truth 'No we have
to use it to mark the gateway of my Ka. I shall quote
it again now we are here' I began
'Oh Geb you are reborn. Only you can read this.
Your enemy now returns from Babylon and brings
the wrath of his king to destroy your chosen
country. Remember the plains of Thebes and the
sacred mountain. Look to the West and the setting
sun and the land of Nut, Queen of the night, and
you will find the place you seek.' I paused and
explained 'When I was looking through the eye, all
I could see was a point about ten metres in front; so
the eye has to lead us the last little bit. It then was
obvious that the words would take us within ten
metres of the point we seek. It would also have to
be a place that has changed little over the many
thousands of years since Yussef wrote his clues for
us. Use the eye of Horus to mark the gateway of
your Ka and the path to heaven. This is the bit I am

not quite sure of, but as we are going uphill are we
on the path to heaven?' I asked because I was
running out of inspiration.

Khalid spoke 'Francis this is called Biban el-Harim,
or as you would say The Valley of The Queens. I
have been here many times over the years. It is
located South of Deir el Medina and West of
Medinet Habu; which I believe you have visited or
should I say sought cover in? I think we are
looking for some ramp over the rock-face in front of
us and not in the valley of the Queens as it has cliffs
all around. It is not possible to see the entrance as
the road turns to go into the valley and in truth we
would be looking west if we go this way.'

He leant over and flashed the headlights so that the
truck leading us was aware of our change of plan.
'Turn left here' he ordered, and the four by four
started up the steeper incline until it reached the top
of the bluff. We all got out and looked down into
the curved valley about twenty metres below. The
lengthening shadows lay on the valley floor now
deep gold in the late afternoon sunlight. Khalid
was pensive; he looked up and down the valley.
The only activity I could see was the archaeological
dig that had obviously been going on for quite a
time. There were permanent looking wood and
galvanised roofed shelters covering several small
digs. Many containers were strewn around amongst

the excavated sandy soil from the many holes. The ancient black mud brick walls stood starkly in contrast with the lightness of the desert; forming a maze like pattern for quite a distance in all directions.

'This has been going on for years Francis.' He said softly. I am sure that there is something not quite right however. I know that the University of Chicago, along with a consortium of other American and International Universities is carrying out these excavations. They have our government's permission and are bona-fide. There may be some irregularities that have gone unnoticed, it is a recipe for intrigue and exploitation. In fact it could be a good cover for the CIA or any clever organisation that wanted to explore the area'

He went to the Toyota and withdrew an attaché-case. From it he extracted the two silver boxes I had hidden from him previously. He placed them upon the bonnet of the vehicle, which was making little noises as it cooled down and proceeded to assemble them and set the antenna to search for a satellite. As you know Francis, both Mossad and the CIA use these so I am thus suspicious of any American or Israeli involvement.

I began to be less naive at this point as a bit of common sense prevailed. I asked 'Do you really

think that The Americans and Israelis were using
me to lead them to the tomb to rob it?
'Francis it is immaterial to either of them who
actually gets there first as long as it is not Malik.
They do not care if you find it or not as long as
Malik does not. They would destroy the tomb or
you. If they alone find it they would remove all
evidence and carry the treasures away as profit to
be hidden in some rich man's vault. If they could
not loot it for whatever reason they would destroy
it. I would destroy it if I felt Malik was about to find
it. This is all about power politics and the
involvement of men in a war of conjecture. They do
not want you to lead the wrong persons there and
they will kill you if they feel you present a risk. It is
not the contents they seek. It is the power they lose
if things do not go the way they want. I believe that
there are many people seeking your tomb, but all
for the wrong reasons.'
But to do this in secret is nigh on impossible
without we Egyptians finding out; thus it must be
done in the open to divert suspicion. This is the
only dig within many miles from here and it has
been going on for a couple of years now. You see
there must be people who believe the legend of the
struggle between Horus and Set has some historical
truth behind it, that it might be based on fact,
however unlikely that might be.'

I was stunned by the implications behind Khalid's reasoning.

'How long do you think others have known of the tomb?' I asked.

'Now that is an interesting question Francis, you see that since it involves governments and superpowers they have access to a myriad of information and facilities. I believe one of the scrolls that Yussef wrote about got into the hands of someone that could decipher some of it or at least realise its significance possibly this enemy of which has been looking already. Do not forget Yussef said that he had placed many clues so that not all could be lost. Or it may be just bad luck that put your picture out into the black market; with the means to lead them all to you. Even if they could not read the hieroglyphics, the cartouche is the same. They at least could put a face to the name even if they were unable to say it.'

'I feel that the Americans and Israelis were running around Egypt chasing these terrorists. It is obvious that they did not want to involve us Egyptians for reasons known only to them.'

Khalid now smiled as hi agile mind caught a thread of thought. 'Remember Francis, it was the Russians who tipped us off regarding an Egyptian group interested in getting an atomic weapon. Why

they did, I am not sure but it may have been
through true concern.
I must say that what he was saying was making
sense as I watched him adjust the unit and turn it
on.
A tone came from it, punctuated by the sound of
voices in a language I did not understand.
'I was right' Khalid said 'that is Hebrew and they
are asking for confirmation and call sign but it is not
us they are calling. It is a shame we cannot hear the
other side of the conversation. I just wonder how
many of them there are out there'
We listened for a few minutes and it was obvious to
Khalid that the messages were for more than one
person as the voice was demanding that different
codenames reply. I became aware of the
implications that they were agitated because of
something urgent. Could it be our presence here?
'My friends it is now plain that time is running out
for those who are against us. I am sure they know
we are here and will soon strike. ' Anna asked if
this meant we were near the tomb and I had to
agree that it looked that way.
The valley wall which rose almost vertically to our
left curved crescent shaped towards us. It reminded
me of a lunar crater that had a tear in one edge. It
was through this gap that the entrance road ran.
Because a higher promontory of sandstone stood

taller than the rest of the western ridge, the shadow lying on the valley floor was thus lenticular or lens shaped, with a long finger pointing from it towards the opposite cliff. It reminded me of an eye. I was not the only one to realise its significance, as we all saw it simultaneously and yelled 'The eye of Horus!' The finger pointed to a solitary tomb beside a large-scale archaeological excavation right by the tarmac road. I could see nothing to denote the hidden repository of Geb. It had to be here but was our interpretation of the clues correct?

Well the shadow could not have changed for thousands of years anyway. Yussef could have stood here and seen the same thing. His words did describe it well.

Returning to the vehicle we now made our way down the slope and after a hurried conference with Imir, we drove into the defile and thus into the valley of the queens. Leaving our transport we walked up to the tomb, now almost totally in shadow and walked around it. I was not convinced I had been correct but felt something deep in my subconscious. Perhaps it was here?

Khalid now gave us a little talk on the history of the place. 'This is the tomb of Queen Thiti from about three thousand years ago. It has been used as a stable and was plundered a long time ago but over there is the tomb of Prince Amon-her-Kopechef

who was a son of Ramesses the third and strangely
it is dedicated to Horus and his four sons Hapi,
Amset, Duamutef and Kebensenuf. I wonder if that
means anything? I again looked through the eye.
The setting sun, the pyramidal mountain and the
tomb were superimposed. This was it!
I looked at the tomb he was indicating; there was no
door. A granite lintel with the carved outstretched
wings welcomed us inside. The polished red granite
floor was worn by the many feet that had brought
the abrasive sand within, and which had also
ground the step away. I could see the work carried
out by those who had restored the tomb. Missing
parts of the plaster had been filled in with light-
grey gypsum to support the precious remnants of
the original wall paintings. Large acrylic sheets
protected them; they kept poking fingers away
whilst allowing the beauty to be seen.
I wondered what I could hope to find that had not
been discovered before. This was surely a dead end,
if you will excuse the pun. I must have got things
wrong. No, the shadow had pointed us here. The
eye showed this tomb. It must be here, but where?
'Well Francis' Khalid asked. I'm sure it must be
near but I have no idea where or what we are
looking for.' I replied despondently. 'Try and put
yourself into the mind of that fellow Yussef then. If
this tomb were here when he moved your Ba into

this valley, then it would not have been touched because the priests believed it bad luck and not pleasing to the gods to disturb the dead and bury others.

I kept on saying the words I had learnt that had brought us here and attempted to put them into perspective in an attempt to tie the clues to a specific position.

'I Yussef, your Head of State, placed your Ba in the sacred ground to return when the sands of time are almost spent. I left with you the power you now seek. I pray your heart is no heavier than the feather of truth and that your Ka walks with the gods'

As I looked at the doorway I thought that I could see a discrepancy between the height of the floor and the outside ground level. There was a slight crack beside the doorstep. 'Can we get a crowbar in here to lever the doorstep?' Khalid went to the vehicle and withdrew an iron bar over a metre long and came back to me. 'What do you want me to do? Have you seen anything my friend?' 'Yes Khalid, I want you to see if the step moves at all. I m not sure why I ask but if anyone can do it, you can'

He smiled at me the sun was setting and it gave him an eerie look. He inserted the Iron bar into a gap in the corner and proceeded to apply his weight against it. Anna and I stood beside him. There was a grinding noise as the step plus a large amount of red granite swung outwards from the wall. Khalid fell back and my first impression was that he had started an earthquake. The ground shook and heaved. We were falling; I grabbed hold of Anna and the world turned upside down.

Chap 25

Everything was moving; the underlying sand was pouring like it was a gigantic hourglass, into the hole. We were trapped in a current that tore the breath from our bodies and infiltrated our mouths, nostrils and every part of our clothing dragging us down into oblivion. It was useless even trying to cry out in case we too became filled with the fine dusty brown powder. I held onto Anna as though she was a life raft, believing full well that if we were separated now, it would be forever. We hit the vortex and accelerated through the narrowing gap and went into freefall for what seemed like an eternity. I landed on a mound of sand; Anna collapsing on top of me tore my breath from my body. We rolled down its sloping sides, over and over like Easter eggs. This broke our fall like sledging down a sand dune. We both came to an abrupt halt against a rock face at the bottom. I lifted Anna's head to stop her from breathing in the dust that cascaded all around us. A shaft of light shone through the hole about fifteen metres above our heads and in its glare I saw Anna looking like an apparition, covered as she was in the fine dust that clung to the perspiration on her face. She opened her eyes; the contrast against the brown covering made her look like a panda. I found it funny and despite the throbbing pain in my healing shoulder, which the fall had aggravated, I started to laugh; she seeing a reciprocal sight, started to laugh also. We were interrupted by the light from above being almost extinguished by the heads of Khalid and Imir having been thrust into the hole to see how we were. When they realised that we were both unhurt, their laughter also rang out and reverberated in the chamber

It was a surreal experience to see the last of the orange gold laser-like sunbeams which cut straight through the motes of dust still suspended in the still air of the chamber, throwing the silhouettes of our comrades demon-like upon the sandstone wall opposite which we still lay. I suddenly saw something indistinct upon the wall. I shouted to them to let the light in. They promptly withdrew and for a few seconds the final rays of the sun entered like golden fire. They bounced off a metal plate set into the side of the hole we had fallen into. It was as though the finger of Ra was pointing. It served to illuminate an orifice in the face of the seemingly featureless rock wall opposite. The low angle of the setting sun had shown the way as promised by Yussef. I quickly took off my belt and laid it out from the point from which I stood so that it would show the direction of what I now believed to be the hidden entrance. Like a spent match, the

light was gone as the sun slipped behind the
Theban hills casting us into darkness and into the
realms of Nut the goddess of night. We both stood
where we were as the darkness fell solidly into the
chamber. I could feel her warm and anxious against
me as we waited for Khalid and Imir to organise
our rescue. I felt that there had been enough
traumas for the moment; this was obviously not
going to be easy if the first few metres were as hairy
as this.

Soon a rope ladder was lowered and our friends
joined us on the sloping floor their torches shone
out into the room and picked out a few chunks of
masonry lying around. They had brought two
haversacks with water, torches and a length of rope
slung around Khalid's shoulder.

There was a huge pile of sand in the middle like a
giant cone; it was this that had saved Anna and I
from being smashed to pieces by our fall.

This chamber was man made but what purpose did
it serve?

Was this the place we had been looking for? It had
to be. There were no inscriptions or statues, just
hewn blocks of stone, granite by the look of it.

What was it doing here?

This was a shale covered limestone and sandstone
wadi. It certainly was not a tomb. Had it been
visited before and plundered?

Were we to learn anything from it? I got the
impression that it had been some form of giant silo
or storage building unlike the formalised temple
and tomb structure I was used to.

Without wood, the ancient Egyptians had resorted
to the natural material, stone.

Not having the arch, which had been invented by
the Romans to great effect, they had been unable to
span large distances, and so had to use many pillars
to hold up the large lintels they were forced to use.
This resulted in the floor space being cluttered by
the sheer number of pillars as at Karnak in the
hypostyle hall.

Here, we were in a very large space, but there were
no pillars to hold the roof up. What then was
actually serving that purpose?

This chamber was like a bottle lying on its side at
an angle of about forty-five degrees and we had just
slid down the neck. There were stone blocks set into
the wall forming a circle where we stood. It was like
being in the bottom of a well.

The rest of the wall appeared to be natural stone
with the occasional block or two, set in it for some
reason or other. I looked at them and was perplexed
by their being there at all.

My second belief came into play here. Why would
the builders put them there except for a purpose?
What were they trying to tell me? There were five of

them, four small blocks and one large block with
they eye of Horus carved upon it. They appeared to
be spread in a random pattern. I used my torch to
examine the rock and all at once it was obvious
what they were. I was looking at the Planet Saturn
with its four moons. It was just as it had been
portrayed on the box. We were truly in the right
place.

Unless we had found the small entrance we would
have had to tunnel through solid rock to this deeply
hidden chamber below.

No wonder it had defied detection. We had to have
had specific directions to the entrance, as there was
no other way to enter. It was incredible that we had
found it at all.

I took a torch and proceeded to take out the reel of
fishing line I had bought in Cairo. Tying it onto a
piece of stone I then picked up my belt making sure
that the line it had marked was not erased by
scuffing the dusty floor with my foot to mark the
direction of the point I had noticed. I did not want
to lose my trousers either. 'What are you doing
Francis? This is no time to be adjusting your
trousers' Asked Anna.

'I'm restoring my belt I used it to mark out
something and to be quite sure I don't really know'
I replied still slightly winded. 'I think that I saw
something over there and I wish to make certain

that I can find it again. I will tell you about it in a minute when we have some more light.'

'How large is this place?' Anna asked. Imir replied 'It is gigantic and seems to be actually hewn from the limestone rock. I have never seen anything like it before. It must be at least forty feet by the same again. I wonder what purpose it served?'

Khalid being the inquisitive one started asking his own questions. 'I think we should be looking for the reason it is built here and nowhere else.' He phrased it like a fictional detective, as though he already knew the answer. 'It is at the bottom of a valley and could have been constructed by just roofing over a section to provide a large sheltered area. To be quite honest with you, it looks as though it is a naturally eroded cavern that has been tidied up a little to serve a purpose.'

He indicated with his massive hand and commented as though he was conducting a grand tour. 'Look at those blocks repairing the wall over there. The roof is possibly salt. Never the less, it is an interesting place to be, especially as we have been led here. It is obvious why it has not been discovered before? Let us stay together and do a little exploring. May I suggest that we all look after Francis, as he seems a little accident-prone.'

I was in no mood to argue with his sentiments; my body now felt like I had won the Grand National carrying a camel.

 I was sure that I was covered in bruises all over and that I would need another holiday far away from here when, or more likely if, we ever got out of this place. I really wanted to finish the job and forced myself into action.

'Come on let's get going I said.' I followed my friends. Imir led the way with his torch and Khalid walked beside Anna. We made our way to the wall opposite around the big sand heap and I was unable to locate the place that the reflected sunbeam had illuminated by just looking.

 For several minutes I scanned the surface. The rock looked featureless and flat, tool marks of the ancient masons were barely visible in the limestone. There was no possible indication that there could be some method of going further. But for my drawing the line from our start point, I would never have seen the niche.

There it was, just like any other bump, except it was meant to be there. What did it do? It was, about a metre above my head. I ran my hand as high as I could; I was only just able to feel a slight edge where two blocks joined. I let my fingers follow the almost imperceptible line and realised that it also ran vertically upwards as though there was a corner. I was getting frustrated. The whole structure was solid and there was no way. To my left, a tunnel sloped down into the bedrock blocked by a jumble of stone blocks that had obviously been dislodged by water at some time. I thus had to lean uphill slightly to keep myself level. It would have been normal for us to follow the corridor along but why then mark the wall about here?

I could feel that I had been here before but it was like trying to remember the name of something or an elusive answer to a question that you really felt you knew but had forgotten. It was bugging me and causing a lot of inner frustration.

I had to accept that it might be possible to get some help from my spiritual self but it was hard to do. No man in his right senses wants to give up control of himself and I don't mean an alcohol or drugs induced trip here. I mean a sudden jolt back into some indistinct past life and a physical trauma when you know that you are not yourself any more but I had to bring Geb to help me. I willed him up, out of the depths of my soul.

I felt myself go giddy and the strange feeling of my other persona started to possess me once again. My voice grew husky and I heard myself speak.

'I have gathered together your Powers. Now I have directed the Powers of the ways, the guardians of the horizon, and of the House of heaven to lead

you. I have established their weapons and
protection for Horus.

I have prepared the ways for him. I have
performed the things, which he had commanded. I
see you Geb. I speak to him concerning the matter
of his Great Son, whom he loves, and concerning
the smiting of the heart of Set.

I look upon the lord who was helpless. How shall I
make them to know the plans of the gods, and that
which Horus did without the knowledge of his
father Osiris?

Travel thou on thy way safely, cry out the gods of
the Heavens to me. O you, who make your names
great in the eyes of the Gods who are chiefs in your
shrines, and who are guardians of the House of
Osiris, grant, I pray you; that I may come to you.

I have bound up this place within itself. Let you
open up the way.'

I jerked back into the present and knew that this
was going to be difficult without a lot of thought.
I could feel that my alter ego was still managing to
control me.

'What are those granite blocks doing lying around?'
I asked, 'Bring them here'. My friends looked at me
as though they thought I was mad but complied
with my request. The blocks were dragged or
carried towards where I stood.

 I was unsure why I wanted them at all but soon there were six, four small and two large lying at my disposal. I could vaguely see the solution but where to start?

Chap 26

'All right everyone; we have a sign on the wall over there. I think it is Saturn and its four moons. Look at the eye of Horus on the big block. We have six blocks here but why? Is anything written on any of them.' Khalid and Imir turned each block over and over to expose the various faces. 'Yes there is' said Imir turning over a large block. 'Here is the eye of Horus' I looked at it and could not fail to realise that it was the left eye. 'Is there an eye on the other larger block?' I asked. 'Yes Francis, and it is the right eye.' replied Khalid. 'I am glad of that'. Said Anna. 'I would have been worried if we had not got a balance, one is evil and the other good.' She was manipulating one of the remaining four. 'There is something written on this small block too! What does it say Francis?'

I looked at the writing that had been crudely scratched on the stone it said beware your enemy is here. As more were exposed the warning was repeated on each one. I had to bluff this one out. There were only the four of us so who could it be? I decided to lie my way out of this one and simply told my companions that these were the clues to set things up. I realised that this was actually the truth. If I stacked the blocks with the warnings together I would have two piles of two and be left with the two large blocks. Perhaps they would form steps.

Why would I need them except to reach the niche I had detected? 'Place them here in front of the wall. Put the big one with the left eye pointing downwards here'. I said indicating the lower part of the floor that tilted downwards. Once that had been done, two others were placed on top, with the other two stacked beside them giving a platform about a metre high. I climbed up and was able to feel the grooves in the wall. What did I have to do now? I tapped the surface. A slight reverberation told me that it was hollow I jumped down and asked Khalid to lift the larger remaining block. He hefted the forty-kilogram weight with ease. 'Now get up onto the step and use it to smash the wall in front of you.' We assisted him as he stepped up onto the blocks and he raised the heavy stone, bringing it down onto the surface with a sound of an earthquake. The wall disintegrated and a hole appeared large enough to get through. 'It was only plaster. The opening is smooth.' He said as he climbed up and through. 'I will use this block as a step on the other side.'
We all followed him into the entrance and found ourselves in a cave like area. The rear of the wall that had hidden this portal was bare and I could see it was made of the same blocks as the rest but these had served to hide the way. Normally you would look for a doorway at ground level, not two metres

off the floor. We had to bend low to exit through
another hole that led us into a narrow man-made
corridor but at least we could stand up. The tunnel
curved like a roller coaster; the sides seemed to
twist so that the perspective was skewed. I
wondered why the builders had done this. Then I
realised that we were actually following a natural
fissure in the earth beneath the Valley of the
Queens. All the artisans had done was to cut the
walls at right angles to the floor. This meant that
sometimes we had to lean on the walls because the
floor tilted about forty degrees. At the same time we
were also either climbing or descending quite
steeply. I followed the others; my fishing line was
running smoothly as the plastic reel gyrated around
my finger. I occasionally snagged it as I used the
same hand to steady myself. The filament was
difficult to see in the torchlight but I was secure as
long as I held the reel. I knew we could return.
After a few minutes we came to a rough-hewn
staircase that led at right angles to the direction we
were taking. There was a carving of the spread
wings on the white limestone rock. The contours of
the sculpture having been accentuated by the
application of some black pigment gave it an
embossed look. It certainly stood out against the
wall. Khalid led the way up the stairs, which started
to turn to the left as though we were ascending a

spiral staircase. A vertical pillar that looked like a
stalactite ran upwards on my left. I marvelled that
whoever had built this tunnel had certainly used
the natural features to facilitate its construction. It
was obvious that we were now beneath the cliffs
that were surrounding the Valley of the queens.
This would never have been found, even if you
spent a millennium or two looking for it.
The steps ended and we all stood on a landing
about three metres wide with a smooth floor. There
was a sort of cave here with writing on the walls. I
stood there with Imir who directed his torch so that
I might read whatever I could. Khalid and Anna
entered the chamber and were ferreting around as I
spoke the words that I had read before in Cairo and
that had impressed themselves into my mind at the
entrance. 'Travel thou on thy way safely, I have
established their fortresses for Osiris. I have
prepared the ways for him. How shall I make them
to know the plans of the gods, and that which
Horus did without the knowledge of his father
Osiris?'
I wondered exactly why this had been repeated. It
had to be for a reason but my mind would not
grasp the significance of what was being
communicated. 'Hey come and look at this you two'
Khalid shouted. 'What is it?' Imir replied 'Come on
Francis; let us see what is going on. You can

examine these later.' I nodded agreement and followed him. Our footsteps were crunching on the smooth surface as we went across to where Khalid and Anna were looking at something off to the right of the chamber.

There was a statue of a cow made of black wood set upon a small dais in front of a continuation of the tunnel; barring the way like some kind of watchdog. It stood about a metre high at the shoulder and the head was covered in gold leaf. The horns spread and rose a further metre and held a disc that represented the sun between them. 'It is Hathor but why is she here?' My mind was now racing. There was something I knew but I could not remember exactly what it was supposed to mean. Beneath the curtain of obscurity I positively knew. I had stood here before; I was sure of that but why couldn't I remember? This was important and deadly. I must remember what it meant. The phrase 'Who are guardians of the House of Osiris, grant, I pray you that I may come to you' kept running through my head. I was being warned; there was definite danger. The phrase 'Fortress of Osiris' came strongly to mind. Fortresses have protection.

I sensed a slight tremor in the air. 'Get down now' I shouted at the maximum amplitude I could possibly produce; panic in my voice giving my words more meaning. We all dropped to the floor, Khalid being the last to fall.

Before the echo of my yell had subsided, a snapping noise then a rushing sound engulfed us as a two metre long projectile reflecting the torchlight; hurtled into the chamber cutting the air centimetres above our prone forms. It hit the top of the staircase and fell rattling downwards chipping off large chunks of rock. It was a close thing; I wanted to be sure that none of us had been hurt and also to see if another Bronze Age cruise missile was on its way so I repeated my original warning but quieter this time. We lay prone for a few minutes and I got up carefully as did my companions. We retrieved the torches and crouched against the walls as a means of protecting our backs. 'Is everyone ok?' I asked I received affirmatives from all and felt relief that no damage had been done. I noticed blood on the white floor and suggested that someone had been hit. On examination it turned out that Khalid had the misfortune to have had the seat of his pants grazed by the missile. It had torn the fabric of his suit and scratched his ample posterior. 'You have the skid marks to prove it now' I laughed.

'What do we do now? Is it safe to go on?' Khalid slowly thought aloud. 'I feel that it is.' I replied ' the writing is a warning that we must not ignore. I will go on ahead so don't trip over my fishing line. It might be the only way back.' I took a torch and led the way carefully into the exit tunnel. Stopping to examine the booby trap, I was amazed at the simplicity that had waited for thousands of years to spring the deadly projectile. A pendulum with a large weight hung into the corridor. A clay wedge that had been restrained by a pot full of sand had held it back. Something we had done had broken the pot and allowed the sand to escape. The hammer had fallen and struck the missile, which had rested in a grooved clay stand that now lay broken on the floor. It had projected it with sufficient force and velocity to kill anyone who stood in its path.

'We might learn something from this. They were really devious back then' Anna was also marvelling at the engineering. I felt that we might have overlooked something important and requested a few seconds for thought. The message said that the guardians were also assistants in finding the way. Hathor was a friendly deity and therefore might be instrumental in our search. 'How heavy is that statue? Is it possible to bring it with us?' Imir answered me since he was the nearest to it. He manipulated the horns and rocked it side to side and back and forth finally lifting it from the dais. 'I would say it is about twenty kilograms no more Francis. Why would we want to drag it along?' 'I

am not sure but I feel it might be a good idea' I
replied. ' I shall bring it; let us get along we have
waited too long here and time is passing' Khalid
said, lifting the statue, tucking it under his arm as
though it was a balsa wood model and striding
towards me along the corridor.

I proceeded to go forward and shone the light to
examine the way. More writing depicting my name
was spaced at regular intervals along the walls and
we made remarkable progress as the path led on
downwards with the erratic tilting as before. I had
needed to tie on another reel of fishing line to the
first as it was running out. We had thus come half a
kilometre from the entrance. It had seemed to be at
least twice that but the convolutions of the tunnel
gave the impression that it had been further.

After an age of panting and sighing we emerged
into a larger chamber. The temperature here was
quite high; we thus were sweating and covered in
dust. Khalid put the Hathor statue down and
stretched himself. He was obviously feeling the heat
too. I sat on its back, resting against the wall; my
armpit was hurting as the sweat trickled into my
bandages and irritated the wound. Anna looked at
me compassionately. 'Are you aright Caro?' I
muttered that I was just a bit out of condition and
tired. 'Where are we?' Anna then asked, I replied 'I
have no Idea but it looks interesting anyway.'

From my sitting position I was glancing around
from a different perspective and as I looked up at
the roof. I could see something above our heads.
Anna followed my gaze.' What is that? She was
pointing to a sort of carving that hung from the
ceiling. 'Can we have some light up here please?' I
asked. Khalid shone the light upwards and I was
able to make out a symbol that looked like the
astrological sign Libra. There were stars on either
side and it had obviously been done in a hurry, as
the quality of the carving was inferior to any we
had seen previously. 'Let's get on, It is nothing' Said
Imir. 'We are taking too long here and we must be
close now' I agreed but I still had those strange
feelings of unease. The General took off into the
chamber and after a few seconds he shouted 'Bring
another torch here.' We looked and I could see his
shadow against the white walls. Khalid held his
Maglite and directed it towards Imir; its beam
cutting the darkness like a Samurai sword and
eventually touching the object of his attention.
Anna helped me to my feet. We made our way
towards where Khalid was standing. There in a
trench set into the floor was a stone crocodile. The
workmanship was perfect. Every scale and detail
down to the claws and teeth was portrayed and
brought the beast to life. I could almost see it
breathing. 'It must beat least five metres long' I said

in amazement 'what does it mean? Also why would anyone go to so much trouble to put something like this here?'

'Are we in a zoo now' said Anna 'this is strange' I felt that there was more than a superficial significance to the statue but I was unable to discern what it could be. Another dim memory floated into my subconscious and fluttered about. The Judgement of Thoth! Sebek was the eater of the heart. There was danger here. 'Get out! Go back!' My voice reverberated all around us as we scrambled in unison to get away from the statue. By now everyone trusted my judgement without question. Anna and I were nearly back at the Hathor statue and as far as I knew at that moment with Khalid and Imir in close pursuit.

Khalid grunted something that seemed like a curse as he fell towards me; I grabbed hold of him to stop him falling into Anna and flattening her against the wall. As I did so I noticed that the floor we had been standing on was no longer there; it had tilted and fallen away. Realising that this could be fatal to my friend I deliberately fell backwards into the tunnel we had recently exited with Khalid half on top of me. The pain shot through me as my wound yet again was knocked but I would never let him go. Anna realising our predicament grabbed hold too and our combined efforts held the big man from

falling into the hole that had appeared. He
scrambled to his feet and picked us both up
hugging our frail bodies to him. 'Allah be praised
for such good people. Thank you my friends.'
 I just had to sit down again because of the awful
pain in my side; in fact I had to lie down again as it
was like a stitch.
I looked around; Imir was further up the tunnel but
at the opposite side across the gap from us clinging
hold to the head of the statue. He was obviously
shaken, but it was difficult for me to see much as
the torches had been dropped and one had fallen
into the void. The other lay where it had rolled; its
beam reflected obliquely off the roof of the tunnel.
It did however give sufficient light to know we
were all alive.
 I just lay there, winded but intact, grateful that my
friends were safe. 'Hey! Get me out of here' Imir
shouted scrambling upwards to safety.
It was obvious that we had tripped another booby
trap; the floor had hinged downwards like a hatch
leaving a gap of over two metres. I knew that if I
could retrieve the torch, I would be able to
understand exactly what had happened. I removed
the spool of line from my finger and placed it on the
floor. 'Hold on Imir, I will be with you in a moment'
I called.

'I would appreciate it if you hurried up Francis, I am getting cramp holding on here.' I reached out my arm and caught hold of the torch directing it towards him.

The tunnel where he stood had come to a dead end and led nowhere. He was stranded on a ledge that comprised the statue of the crocodile, plus a couple of metres of stone floor. He was thus in no immediate danger but I supposed from his perspective without sufficient light to see it could look far worse than it was. I would not have wanted to jump this gap without much of a run up either. Khalid and Anna were farther up the entrance tunnel than I, so I crawled to the edge of the pit and looked down to where the second Maglite lay on a ledge about six metres down. It was still shining and I could see in its beam that there was a second tunnel on the left running at right angles to the direction we had been travelling, about half way up. It would never have been visible from above.

 I must have disturbed a stone because it fell into the pit and hit the torch below sending it spinning into the depths where it bounced off the walls and was finally extinguished. It must be at least thirty metres deep.' I gasped.

I now retreated from the edge and stood up. Khalid and Anna joined me as we scanned the gap for a way to retrieve Imir. There were distinct hand and footholds in the walls and by the use of these along with our shouted directions, Imir returned to stand beside us thankful for his deliverance. It was obvious that those who built this killing machine had to enter and exit during its construction. They had needed to cross the gap too.

'We are going to have to retrace our steps back as there is no way forward' Anna looked disappointedly at me. 'I disagree' I replied, 'There is another tunnel beneath this one. The balance shows that there is equality and the crocodile shows us that it is guarding the underworld. The entrance must be accessible from here. 'Khalid can you lower me down to that ledge; there is another entrance down there.' The big man nodded. 'Not without a rope around you my friend'. He unrolled the cord he had also carried and made to tie it around me. 'Here you are Francis, I have no desire to lose you so please be careful.'

Without further discourse I found myself holding our last torch, standing on the shelf about six metres down from the top. I tried to reach sideways across the gap to the other entrance that had been cut at a sloping angle so that the top hung out like a canopy, hiding it out of sight from above. This protuberance also served to stop any attempt to use a rope as a pendulum as a means of entry.

 Whilst I could touch the wall, I could not get a grip so that I might enter the concealed entrance. Looking down at my feet to see if there were any footholds, I noticed that there were four indentations in the ledge. Their purpose was immediately obvious; Hathor would fit here! 'Can you lower the statue down here please' I shouted upwards. 'What are you trying to do Francis? It is not an art gallery' Joked Imir. Soon the statue rested with its feet securely in the four indentations with the head pointing towards the entrance. I got onto its back and with the aid of the strength of Khalid pulling me upwards, supporting my balance. I was now able to scramble over the lip and to pull myself in.

 The tunnel was smooth and tilted upwards into the solid rock. The surface was slippery but had groves cut into the floor for grip. My feet found purchase and I was in. Shining the torch I could see that this shaft was circular in section and that it curved upwards.

Like a snake I wriggled along on my stomach pushing the torch in front of me and craning my neck to see forwards. After a few more metres the shaft went nearly vertical and it was extremely difficult to make progress.

As I looked up the shaft, I could see something unique in Egyptian Art. I had never seen anything

like it on any wall or in books. All that was
portrayed was a man in flames. What could it
mean? I saw the two great clay seals bearing my
name embossed within its cartouche. They were
untouched. I reached out my hand and my fingers
brushed one. Geb now spoke directly to me.
'Beware! Do not enter by this way. Keep secret the
gateway and seek another by means of Hathor.' I
knew precisely what was meant, for had I not
entered by the left-hand entrance? That always
would be the evil side. I assumed that the booby-
trap set here would be lethal as there would be no
escape from the confines of this tunnel.
There would be another hidden doorway
somewhere on the right. All that remained was to
find it. My torch was noticeably dimmer now and I
was sure that it would be only minutes before the
Nickel metal Hydride batteries gave up their last
few electrons and the Tungsten Halogen bulb its
photons In other words I would be in the dark. Not
an exciting prospect when you have your head up a
shaft and are unsure where the hell your feet are.
 A feeling of great sadness swept through me and
an inner voice told me that I had nearly succeeded
in finding the resting-place of my Ba. I shouted
asking to be extracted from here, not wanting to
remain any longer.

Being unable to turn round, I slowly slid backward using my toes as a brake until my feet exited into the entrance of this tunnel. The light was going fast. Khalid, understanding my predicament and having been alerted by the reappearance of our only light, somewhat dimmer, took up the strain on the safety rope and I popped out like the proverbial cork. After enduring the obligatory pendulum experience I was finally deposited amongst my friends just as the light went.

We all instinctually retreated from the pit. Anna reassured us that she had hold of my fishing line. 'We have Ariadne and her forethought for Theseus in his hunt for the Minotaur for our way out. It is a bit of Greek mythology mixed in with ancient Egyptian mythology.' I said.

'Pass this reel through your belts and grab hold of each other and let us make our way slowly back.' This was more easily said than done because of the nature of the path we had come, but roped together like a bunch of fish; we had the advantage of not losing each other or the way.

Total darkness has the effect of total disorientation. We were constantly banging our heads on the walls and ceiling or stubbing our toes.

It was a frightening experience to descend the staircase. The eight hundred or so metres seemed like a marathon in a ghost train ride.

 Remarkably, we reached the bottom of the staircase and out through the false wall without serious injury.

 Once up the rope ladder I was grateful for a large bottle of water and a chance to breathe fresh air again. I was also trying to understand why the tomb entrance had been constructed like this. We had come through a type of three-dimensional snakes and ladders maze and still were no nearer finding what we sought.

 'I feel that I am losing the plot,' said Khalid as if in response to my thoughts. 'All tombs have entrance tunnels but this beats anything' Anna was as perplexed as anyone was; she held my hand like a lost child. 'Caro let us go back and try again tomorrow' '

Yes let us halt for now' replied Imir. I was glad that the loss of light had prevented the others from seeing all that I had. It also pleased me that for the moment that only I knew that the goal had been reached. It would give me time to sort out my thoughts and come up with a plan to protect against the enemy that Yussef had warned me about

.' I would like to go back to the hotel and get good nights sleep' I yawned'.

'Unless you wish to spend hours getting there and back tomorrow, then I suggest we stay nearby. We have lost too much time already,' Imir said with authority as he ordered several soldiers to guard the opening that Anna and I had fallen into such a short time before.

They moved into position with silence and practised efficiency. They already had got some food on the go and their vehicles were drawn up along the tarmac. We got into the Toyota and settled down as we were driven out of the valley.

Chap 27

The night was well established as we drove south, away from the valley; the broken gravel and sand roadway causing the vehicle to pitch and lurch. My aching body was moaning silently and my head hurt again. We were being taken to a military outpost not far from the escarpment and would spend the night there. Khalid and I sat in the rear of the vehicle with a rather tired Anna in the front seat as we jolted our way.

 The soldier driving was concentrating on not deviating from his path. I would have too if I had to control this machine but I did feel that he was driving a bit too fast for the conditions. None of us wanted further injuries if that could be avoided. The general consensus was that we really should go back to the hotel for a bath and a good nights sleep. Anna mentioned that it was a bit strange that since we could control the entrance to the tomb and that it did not matter how long we took to get back the next day. I agreed but added that there must be a military reason for Imir keeping us away from others because of security, and that I had no desire to be back in hospital again for whatever reason. ' Caro, I feel unhappy about the situation, I do not know why but there is something wrong. It seems to be too much out of control. There is no need for

them to keep you alive any more because they now know exactly where to find the tomb.' 'My sweet you forget that Yussef wrote that only I may enter. There is obviously another grand booby trap that will destroy the tomb and contents, or something of that nature. I have an idea of what it could be but obviously I will have to see what clues Yussef has left me.' ' That fellow must have loved you so much Francis. I wonder why he went to all the trouble to protect something. I also wonder what that something is that it requires so much secrecy?'
'I have no idea except that it must be a secret that could be as valid today as it was all those years ago. Perhaps it is technological or historical; anyway all will be revealed very soon now.' I replied.
' Whatever it is, the value will be beyond price to whoever removes it first but since you must be there, then you are bound to find out' 'That my darling depends on how long I am allowed to live afterwards of course.'
As I said this, I wondered why I had said it at all but I felt a cold shadow pass over the soul of Geb. He was always in my inner thoughts and I realised that I would have to open up and let him guide me a little more now, or else I might not survive too much longer.
When a person does something, he or she must have a logical reason for the decision, logical for

them perhaps. Possibly they also reason out the consequences too. I had always been methodical. It had been the only way to survive in my former profession. Now, I was doing things and not even knowing why. How much of Geb was I? Or how much of me was Geb? I had never known a pharaoh named Geb. So when did he live? How old was he when he died? Was Geb therefore a generic name for all pharaohs? I now felt it could be since they were all sons of Ra. reincarnated. Perhaps in the knowledge of this I could be more definite. Perhaps I may understand who or what I now was. 'One who is known to you!' That had to be the most enigmatic sentence Yussef had left me. I was still unsure how he would or could know the future. Was this all pre ordained and planned like an ever-looping tape?

There were several stories all through history. The battle of good against evil, the legend of Horus and Set and the expulsion of Lucifer from heaven had all shaped our perception of our eternal fate and the direction our soul might take in the hereafter. Religions were based on this supposition so perhaps it has a firm basis. What of reincarnation? There were several eastern religions such as Buddhism that put this as the core of belief. It meant that we physically came back as a non-remembering version of our previous self. The secret had to be communicated somehow because my protagonists had known who I was before I had. How did they have knowledge beyond mine? Perhaps all our roles had been paralleled into the present but I was unsure of the others. What present-day occupations translated backwards? I mean, I had defused bombs and lived by logic. I suppose that some of the qualities were part of the role of a king. So what present parallel could link Malik to me?

After about ten to fifteen minutes we drew up alongside some tents adjacent to a ruined village, which were illuminated by some oil lamps. Khalid got out and I followed. Anna was ferreting around in the front picking up her shoes or something. 'I'll be back in a second I must find a toilet' 'Follow me Francis, so must I' Khalid and I walked away across a dirt road and went behind a half-collapsed dried mud brick wall. 'This will do Francis, it is private enough' he said and started to relieve himself. I followed suit and a couple of minutes later we both returned the way we had come. The vehicle and General had gone and there was no sign of Anna.

Chap 28

Anna had vanished. Frantically we searched the area but it was fruitless. Khalid deployed every man he could find. I ran around helplessly, distraught with the fear and anguish of her loss. How could I have been so stupid? Imir had led us through a maze of intrigue. I should have realised that he had been the one who I had read the warning of in the disks.

It seemed he had betrayed us all by his duplicity. Lies and subterfuge had been his tools to draw us in and find what he sought. We had innocently led him to the tomb. Now poor Anna had become his hostage. She had suspected that not all was what it had seemed, that was why he had taken her. She was the key to getting me to open the tomb. She was the only reason I would do it for them. He would now deliver her to the traitor Malik. It was plain now that he had been working for my enemies all the time. He was however, pretty high up in the general staff and was close to Mubarak. I worried for the president's safety also. How many others were involved?

Why had Imir done this? Was he also two people? I had been sure that he as honourable but I had been wrong. In all the time I had known him he had not rang any alarm bells. He had protected me when I had been weak he had been my guardian, or had it been my observer?

We were trapped here without transport. It had been simple for Imir to leave us. We had been too involved in the solution of the clues to really notice that the soldiers had been re-deployed. It had seemed normal to send out scouting parties and to set up a perimeter for our safety against the potential threat of attack by Malik and his men. The gradual exit of the dozen or so military personnel had gone unnoticed by all of us.

 The very fact that Anna had been with the general had also lulled us into this false sense of security. I felt that the soldiers had been sent back out of the way because they knew how important Khalid was. Most of them had come here with us from Cairo. They knew we had been with the president and they could be trusted to be loyal. The men were obviously being sent back to base in Luxor for the night. This would enable Imir to return with his own men and that character Malik. It would not be long now; night was upon us. I had to find her. What if I could not find her? The thought was unthinkable. Anna had become so much an essential ingredient in my life. Imir had known that and would use that fact to his advantage.' Khalid we must find her quickly before they have the time to regroup. Imir definitely went back to Luxor and

the Land-cruiser left us here about five minutes ago.
I calculate that we have around an hour until he
gets his hands on her. When he does, I am afraid
that I will have to do whatever he wants'.
'She is the bait and they will come for you soon,
Whatever happens we will do all we can to stop
them and save your lovely lady. You must stay here
so that we may protect you. It is obvious that they
cannot succeed without your helping them.
Whatsoever you feel my friend you must put the
lives of all before yourself. That is the price of
kingship and honour' although I hurt terribly
inside, I had to agree with him. Many would die if I
were selfish now.
'I understand dear friend, but I cannot let you do
that. Your judgement is clouded and we as a
country cannot afford to lose this battle' 'But Khalid
I love her so much!' I nearly sobbed. 'Then we must
find her Francis! They went off in that direction, not
quite towards Luxor. I feel they must have set up a
rendezvous point so that they may monitor what
we are doing. When Imir returns, he will seek to
wipe us out. However he will want to use your
powers and thus will need you so I will have to
keep you here. 'I will destroy him' I said in the
ancient tongue. 'I will turn him into sand and
spread him across the desert forever' Khalid
responded sympathetically. 'I think I understand

the sentiment of what you are saying, even if I do not understand the words but will your resolve falter?' 'Khalid, believe me, I shall save her or die in the attempt' 'Alright Francis but do not lose against Malik or the whole world will suffer. I may have to kill you if Malik takes control; it is not what I could have wanted, so go my friend. I shall collect some men and follow. Take my automatic and a couple of magazines. May Allah bless your search and may he grant his will to give you victory. Never fear, I shall be close'

Khalid tried to console me. 'Francis they will not harm her, they will use her to get you to show them the exact location of the entrance. While you have the box, and the knowledge, they will bargain. It is obvious that our locating the area so quickly has forced Imir to act before we could open the tomb ourselves. They will need more time than one night to remove what they need. He handed me the gun he had used to protect me in Luxor. We embraced; great tears ran down his face and glinted in the firelight. 'Go Francis go, before I change my mind' he said quietly. I needed no second bidding and raced off in pursuit of the Land-cruiser. I was praying that we were correct in assuming they had not gone too far. I also prayed that my great friend would not have to kill me either.

As I have always said, I am not a hero. I have never killed before but all that had to change from this moment on. I am not brave but now I have to make that choice. I am analytical but now I have to become callous. Anna needed more from me than the man I had once been. I would ultimately have to pay the true price of my love and protect the woman I loved. I prayed that when the time came my courage would not let us down.

Could I kill a man? I would now try, not in anger but out of an evil necessity. I drew away from Khalid as he searched the village, rounding up his men; I had his gun and I would sort this thing out myself.

From deep within me I was aware that I knew this terrain; I must have lived here at one time. I felt I knew where to go. I could navigate quite well even by starlight. It was like walking around a planetarium. I was able to see the faint sodium glow of Luxor in the distance as the Nile threw up the beams from the streetlights into the night sky aided by the dust from the traffic. This gave me the direction I must take.

Evil is born of selfishness. It requires that the evil one disregards the needs of others and seeks only their own needs or wants without regard to the feelings of anyone else. It might be the drunk driver who kills a child. Did he need to drink knowing the possible consequences of being drunk? He had the choice but did not care. It could be someone tormenting an animal. You see it is easy to be evil. Children do things that are terrible to each other. We usually chastise them, and then forgive them but if left uncontrolled, they can grow up liking what they do to others. Remember that is what power allows you to do, hurt someone. I had always looked upon evil people as carrion that fed upon the misery of others.

I have seen the terrible things done in the name of freedom. I had defused bombs planted by just about every terrorist group there was but I had never experienced the fear of trying to stop a man hell-bent on destroying millions for his own purpose. He was not mad, just evil.

Was I capable of stopping this avalanche of atomic destruction? Why me? I am just a man in love. I keep on telling myself that I am not a hero but now faced with reality, I have to concede that I shall have to become one.

Death is like an eternal persistent hunter who follows us all. If we become weak or careless injured or sick. He pounces and removes our soul. Most of our lives are spent in ignorant fear of him. We feel we can beat him when we are young and his arrival when we are old is often welcome.

I felt him near but I can assure you that I did not
wish to meet him again. Never would be too soon at
present. Having been his victim at least once before,
and nearly again at least twice in the last ten days, I
could not see why it had to be my turn again, nor
was I deluding myself?

I believe that certain things within ones life, like
growing up, growing older and finally growing old,
are adventures all leading to that inevitable final
day. Not all of us have total control but now alone
in this desert prison apart from a foolish mistake,
like putting my hand on a scorpion or snake; I
would bring death to visit my enemies. I would
have no compassion. No longer would I be the
victim. I would become death's helper and take him
as my companion tonight.

I was a warrior once more; I would hunt for Anna
and destroy her kidnappers. Khalid had been right;
we had forced Malik to act by our proximity to the
tomb. I wondered why Imir had turned
treacherous. What had driven him to betray his
president? Was it the fundamentalists? I had liked
him but I had been so innocent. A strange thought
came to me as I remembered the warnings Yussef
had left me. Thank god it had been Imir because the
alternatives were too terrible to contemplate, as the
only other person who met the criteria was one who

was close to me. This was one who I might not fight against.

How barren are our lives without true love. We are the sum total of our emotions and experiences.

All we really own are the memories we hold and when we die are they to be lost?

I am not sure here, but if we can transfer our love to others; they can bear it like a torch down through the generations passing it on as a cherished gift. Of course only those who knew us can relate the stories about our being. They can really describe our love. But what if they were changed by our love? Then it is the love that endures and we as beings pass into history becoming like the faded photographs that mean nothing to our great grandchildren.

Unfortunately it is the evil people who are remembered vividly; they live in folklore and frighten us in dark quiet moments when we are children. They invade our senses when evil acts are perpetrated. They blight our lives. They also take our lives and use them for their own gain; it is they, who are the human predators.

Chap 29

What is love? I feel it is a miracle we love at all,
because of its potential for destruction and gloom.
When it goes well, it enlightens all the senses and
leads me to achieve things that alone and
unmotivated I would never attempt.

When it is reciprocated it gives me a wonderful
insight to my most secret feelings of self and
surroundings. My life had been full of distractions
and I had been living on a day to day basis; what
with the mortgage and sundry expenses, I had been
wasting time for most of my life, just to stand still
financially. I had not gone forward in spirit until
now. I was thus examining my motivations and
assessing my strengths and weaknesses. I felt that I
was going through the conscious removal of my
typical twenty-first century ideology and replacing
it with the true means of human survival.

All these thoughts ran like a continuous river
through my mind as I made my way back towards
the valley of the Queens. I was drawing on my
psyche. As Francis, I had to bring my woman back
but the fight would have to be carried out as Geb.
There had to be an advantage knowing that I had
lived before. I should be wiser than those who had
not. I should be less afraid to die. I should know a
lot about survival. Most important, I should know
the desert and use her to help me. I must now let

my head and not my heart, rule my actions. This is
difficult to say when the object of my love is a
prisoner of my worst enemy. Or that my worst
enemy was; or had been, a friend.

Night wrapped me like a shroud. I felt its coolness
probe my skin like the fingers of death. Everywhere
lay danger and I hoped that I was still able to
combat its challenges. This was the stuff that
nightmares are made of but unfortunately I was
awake. The soil that the Arabs had called Khemi
and from which we got the word alchemy was
barren but beautiful by day. It was schizophrenic
really. It had a different persona once the sun had
set. I suppose like the legend of Horus and Set, each
had control during their own part of the day. Horus
the Hawk riding on the solar stirred thermals by
day and Set moving unencumbered by night. I had
to fight my opponents on their own ground but I
hoped they would not suspect my secret alter ego
helping me.

The proximity to an oasis or water beneath the
surface gave rise to a crust of salt over a black
muddy marshy interior that could give way and
trap an unwary individual. The locals called this
Kavir and avoided it; I hoped that in the darkness I
could too. The normal surface was hard sand and
gravel that I had been reliably informed was called
Dasht. I had plenty of experience with it already. It

was only the risk of turning an ankle and the noise it made, which stopped me racing along.

Because the cold air was denser and there was no background noise except the occasional crack of a rock contracting as it cooled; any noise I was making would travel for long distances and give me away. I noticed that even with no moon; I could still see the faint outlines of my surroundings. If I really stared at a point I was able to see in greater detail. It certainly made me realise how much light there actually was, even miles away from habitation.

I was also aware that I had become soft over the years. At one time I had been extremely fit. I had been reckless and carefree but also calculating. Ordinance or explosives were unforgiving to anybody that took them lightly. They were predictable but deadly. I knew that I had to change so that I would be unpredictable and even more deadly.

I felt the sweat cool my body down. The night air had become much colder. My feet probed the surface and thudded gently down onto the sand as I half ran back towards the Nile. I was trying not to advertise my presence, break an ankle or to fall; I needed to be alert and ready for anything.

Suddenly my nose picked up the acrid smell of tobacco. Turning my head from side to side, I was able to determine the direction from which the smell had come. To my right there was a slight hill about dune size. I crept on all fours up the side. The surface seemed covered by some sort of crust that crumbled as I drew myself up. Thankfully there was no noise. I came to the top and saw the glow of a cigarette as the man drew hard upon it. His face was illuminated but not distinctly. I was able to see his head covering and the AK47 assault rifle around his shoulder. A reflection of his cigarette also touched my retina from something below him. I stared at it and was just able to make out what seemed to be a Land-Cruiser. This had to be one of the enemies; I would not have a second chance. He was just about to die and I would kill him. It would have to be silently because he might not be alone. Like a snake I slowly approached him. He cleared his throat and spat loudly in my direction, again drawing in smoke. I was close enough now to see the reflection of the red tip of his cigarette in his eyeballs. Due to the light of his last cigarette so close to him his night vision did not stretch out to where I lay. I came from behind him and brought my pistol crashing onto his skull. He fell onto his right side and I sat on his head, forcing his face into the sand for what I took to be an eternity. He feebly struggled and lay still beneath me. I looked for a pulse but found none. I felt the tremors of guilt and fear as I came to grips with the ruthlessness of Geb working within me.

Taking his rifle along with a spare magazine. I made my way down the dune towards where I had seen the vehicle. Sure enough another man sat in the driving seat. There was a flash; I dropped to the ground my night vision compromised. What looked like a flame was now flickering from a gas lighter. He too was smoking; I thought that smoking was definitely going to be fatal for him as well and almost laughed out loud. He would be having trouble seeing for a second or two. I leaped to my feet and tore his door open. The interior light came on. He uttered an expletive attached to a name obviously thinking me to be his dead companion and slipped sideways out of the doorway. As his head cleared the door pillar, I brought the rifle, butt first, like a scythe downward on his neck. There was a thump like a pork chop hitting the floor and he died in mid-air. I was getting quite good at destroying my foes. Anton Kalashnikov had designed this simple but effective weapon in 1944. By 1949 the soviet army adopted the Automatic Kalashnikov design of 1947 as their standard rifle. ; Hence its name AK47 and it had brought death in all forms since then. I doubted if I was the first to use it this way. A Webley British Army Second World War service revolver clattered against the

door as it exited along with the dead man. I picked
it up and started to see if I could steal the Toyota.
The key was not in the ignition, 'damn!' I could not
use it to get away. I looked at the man lying dead at
my feet and began searching his pockets.
Behind me the vehicle started to rock and I brought
the revolver up to bear on whoever had been in the
back. A pair of feet started kicking the windows. It
was Anna! I don't know what I really felt at that
moment but as I stuffed the gun into my waistband
and wrenched the door open and pulled her trussed
up body to me, tearing at the rope that bound her
and removing the bag they had placed over her
head. Tears of joy ran down my tired face. This was
a miracle beyond my most optimistic expectations. I
had never thought it would be this easy. I hugged
her closely to me rocking side to side in my
jubilation, the AK tapping the open door as I did so.
A muffled roaring from behind the rear seats scared
me out of my wits and I pulled the AK round to
bear on whatever had made the sound. Anna sat up
and simply said 'Oh that must be Imir' I nearly
died. I went around and opened the rear doors to
see a trussed up package with army boots covered
in blood poking from it. He was obviously
wounded but not fatally. As I released him from his
bag and bindings I saw the extent of his injuries. He
had a broken leg and the bone jutted out from his

ankle. I ripped the shirt off the dead driver, as he would not need it any more and improvised a splint by tying his lower legs together. Imir was unable to go on and we could not leave him for the vengeance of Malik.

It was obvious we would not go far without transport. I instructed Anna to find the key for the Toyota but she informed me that they had simply broken down and the dead men were awaiting rescue from Malik who would be here in a few minutes.

The hatred I had felt for Imir dissolved like a sugar lump in hot tea leaving me with a bitter taste of guilt in my mouth and absolute terror in my heart. I had to restrain myself from bursting into tears as Anna described his valiant, unsuccessful attempt to rescue her from the two men who had lain in wait back at our campsite. They had both been taken as not to alert Khalid, his men and me

. I just stood immobile; the pain obvious on my face illuminated by the inside light of the vehicle. 'What is it Francis? You look as though you have seen a ghost' Anna was really worried 'what is it caro?' There was no alternative now but for me to face the most terrible truth that any man has to face. A truth I had pushed back into the most profound reaches of my mind. I reached into my pocket and withdrew my wallet. From it I took the picture I had carried throughout.

'He is with you always'. How those words stung. I looked at the smile I knew so well, my world folded tightly around me as the realisation bored its way into my reason.

He had sent me here. He had known where and when I would be in Egypt. He had known my very thoughts and habits. Malik had to be Steven, my own son! I would be up against one I loved most dearly.

I felt like breaking into tears and just giving up. The pain was like nothing I had ever felt. It was like a physical and mental beating that I could never get relief from. All the cuts and bruised were inside me and would never heal. This was what hell must be made of but deep inside I knew that this was not the first time I had endured such sorrow. I had been here before. I had been the loser then and the pain had been as real as now.

Geb was controlling me now and I willingly let myself come under his awesome influence. It was like a local anaesthetic, my pain was being shunted sideways somewhat and my reason became more focused on survival and escape than on selfish fatherly feelings.

The sound of a heavier vehicle invaded my grief and I realised that I had to protect my two companions. It would not be much good to start a firefight here as Anna had no experience of weapons, and Imir could not move far from the Land-cruiser.

I would have to draw them off but first I had to hide the General. 'Hurry Anna and carry this gun. If you can see any water then bring it; let's get out of here; now!'

I swung Imir so that his feet dangled over the rear of the vehicle. He cried out in agony as the weight of his foot pulled at the break. Picking him up over my shoulder, I stumbled away over the dark terrain with Anna beside me.

The sound of the engine was getting nearer; it was varying as it climbed towards us. I estimated that we had but minutes before the might of Malik would be visited upon us. I noted that there were many gullies and the Kavir lay around.

I found a hole about two feet deep and laid him in it. 'Stay still friend and you will not be found. I will set up a diversion and draw them away. I caught hold of Anna's hand and pulled her along with me as I made my way back to where my first victim had sat.

Raising the revolver and sighting along its barrel, I fired three shots in quick succession towards where I believed the truck was coming from. The big 38 calibre kicked in my hand and as I hoped, the low velocity rounds hit the vehicle with a reassuring thwack. The engine note ceased. I knew they had heard us so the chase was now on and all we had to lose was our lives. I did not really care about mine, for I had lost my son. Anna however was innocent in this and I would protect her from the devil himself if I had to. So I had to go on.

Chap 30

We ran as though the hounds of hell were on our heels. The fear of the consequences of being caught lent us the speed we needed. My wound hurt and I hoped I would last out long enough. Had there been enough time to heal? The stitched flesh was stinging again due to my sweat under the now restricting bandages; I wondered when it would stop. Life was not exactly ideal at the moment, or would it end tonight?

I kept looking up at the night sky towards Orion, so that we did not run in a circle but straight away from our enemies. There was a shout a long way back, as they discovered the Toyota and thus Anna's escape. It was not long before I heard the noise of pursuit with the starting up again of the truck. The sound carried clearly to us. I estimated our lead to be around half a Kilometre. The heavy vehicle seemed to be coming in our direction. As far as I could tell, they did not have night vision equipment; they did however have guns and other more frightening weapons. There was nothing else to do but run.

The ground now slanted downwards towards the valley floor and this only served to accelerate our progress but at the cost of striking the small, and not so small rocks that had been deposited there by previous flash floods.

It was extremely dark and I decided to take it a bit more slowly after Anna had a bad fall. 'Don't worry about me Francis, I will be alright' she panted as I lifted her tired body. Scouting around, I noticed a deep wadi, a dried up watercourse to our left. It seemed to run in the general direction we were going. 'Get down here' I gasped from lack of breath. I leaped the short distance to the bottom. Anna sat on the edge as the beam from the truck headlights struck the darkness, illuminating the desert around us. I pulled her into my arms and prayed we had not been seen. The beams gyrated and skipped as the truck bounced over the uneven surface. The scrunching noise of the displaced stones sounded sharp and frightening.

I knew why they had used the lights. It was to avoid this and other gullies. Malik was trying to second-guess our actions. It would be obvious to him that someone had to have rescued Anna. There was no way she could have escaped unaided from the vehicle in which she had been trapped. It had needed someone else, to free her. It was obvious that it had to have been me. I was the subject of his trap and he would be more than mad with me now especially as I had killed two of his men.

I wondered what Steven was thinking. How long had he known that Geb was his father in the present? What had driven him to get me here? I had certainly been influenced to visit Egypt at this time by him. He had insisted I come here. Was that because he knew who I was? I certainly had not known and perhaps I would never have known without the presence of the artefacts and the other persons from my past. I wondered when he had become aware of his past persona. He had never shown any real interest in Egypt other than the normal school homework. He had always wanted to work in the petrochemical industry. Perhaps it had not been chance that he worked in Iran. Perhaps he too had been made aware of the person he had once been. I prayed that I was wrong but the fact that I always carried his photograph with me; thus he was always with me as Yussef had tried to warn me from the start and that he was close to me; were very convincing. How many times had I skirted around what Geb had been trying to communicate through our shared soul? My original surmise about when the reincarnated Ka lets you actually become aware that you are reborn; struck me as ironic. If I could be Geb then it followed that my son could parallel the past and might be my Prime Minister as the Papyrus in Cairo had hinted. It was logical but was it possible?

Since Geb was a generic name, then who was I
really? As hard as I could, it was not possible for me
to comprehend the magnitude of my unwelcome
situation. Steven was my son. My love for him was
unshaken but I really had a responsibility to all the
others he would destroy. It was not exactly what
any father would desire. To have a son who wanted
to kill him. Would he believe that I would fight
him? Would he have harmed Anna? Or did he want
to force me to help him achieve his aim by using
her?

What would he do? What would I do in his place? I
would seal off this little valley and beat backwards,
driving Anna and myself in the opposite direction
to that we were going in now. To do that however
he would have to get in front of us. It would not be
difficult in a truck. That was why they put the lights
on. He needed speed and would sacrifice
concealment to achieve it. This I resolved would be
his greatest mistake. I had been trained for combat
and understood the principles of ambush. I had
never however, put any of the theory into practice
and had the added fact that failure meant death to
Anna and myself. I did have a slight advantage; I
knew my enemy, up to a point that is but I did
know his motive. I would never underestimate him
either.

If we could get to their start off point, we could
break the line easily before it was properly
deployed. But where would it begin? We rested for
a few moments savouring the time as we filled our
tired lungs with the cool night air. As we did so, it
was possible to look over the edge of the wadi
where we were standing as it was only about a
metre and a half deep and follow the general
movement of the truck as it now drew away in front
of us. We however had the advantage that we could
cross at any point we wished. They had to go the
long way round, as they could not cross the trench -
like defile except at its source, or where it ended.
The sliver of the waning moon was ascending but it
would give very little light. I then noticed that we
had another advantage, they were silhouetted
against the crescent; so we could track them when
they stopped.
Hand in hand we ran down the gradient, stopping
occasionally to see if I had opened my wound, ever
watchful for the truck. It stopped about two
hundred metres in front of us and then turned into
what appeared to be another wadi that branched off
this one. They were reversing it into what seemed
to be a tight gap. I could tell by the movement of the
headlights. They were trying to conceal it from us.
They had no idea we were this close or they would

not be doing three point turns and creating so much fuss.

I now estimated that the situation would take about five minutes to develop. It would take that time to deploy the men into some form of skirmish line and commence the sweep back up the valley. Malik would place the men about ten to fifteen metres apart in a wide line across the valley neck. If we knew where the outmost person was, we could get around the outside and thus escape the net. There would be a danger however, that a lone individual might be placed behind the line to cut off this route of escape. I hoped they had decided on the move and not got the time. The outer man was climbing the sides of our wadi getting into position. He could look down upon us if we continued much further. If there had been more light it would have proved dangerous for us anywhere. All we had to ensure now was that we made no noise to indicate we were this close to them.

Chap 31

Silently we also ascended the sloping sides, under
the cover of the noise Malik and his party were
making. Orders were being whispered and
weapons cocked. I extracted my 9mm pistol; the
AK47 was not going to be much use at this range,
we were too close. I slid back the mechanism to
bring a round into the breech. I lowered the
hammer gently and silently moved the safety catch
off with the ball of my thumb. All I need do was
cock and fire. I had no wish to do that at this time,
as it would mean instant discovery and certain
death for us both.

I stuck the weapon inside my shirt; it must not
reflect the slightest moonbeam.

We crawled out of the wadi and onto the rim
praying that no stones would fall to give us away.
Slowly Anna and I made our way to outflank the
outer man. What we had not noticed in the near
total darkness was that the ground rose again in
front of us in the form of an escarpment. If we were
to climb, we would displace a lot of shale and thus
give our position away. We were trapped; it was
impossible to outflank the line. The man came
further in our direction as the sweep began. If we
were to retreat now it was certain others who
would be walking up the wadi floor would catch us

in minutes. It was not an option; it was down to fortune now.

Anna whispered 'I can see a hole, over there!' We moved towards a darker patch of ground about five metres in front of us and lay down in the slight depression in the sand. It would provide some cover but would not stand close inspection.

The darkness wrapped itself around us like a black velvet curtain as we huddled together keeping ourselves close to the ground as to avoid being seen. The sound of footsteps scrunching along the ground, the clink of weapons and whispering grew closer as the group hunting us started to spread out. It would be only a matter of seconds before we were discovered and in my imagination; I could almost feel the blow of the impending bullet; I knew from recent experience, the likely effect. Time seemed to pass with incredible slowness as we lay there awaiting our fate I recalled the last occasion I had relied upon the night to save me. This time there was far less light but less cover too. I strained to see the nearest man, the sand had stuck to the sweat on my cheek and grit had made my eyes sore. I barely saw him; just a dim outline standing about three metres away, he was looking around and seemed to be reliant more on his ears than his eyes.

Suddenly Steven shouted my name; his anger and
frustration were extremely obvious. I would
recognise his voice anywhere; all my doubts
evaporated at that moment. I could not deny the
truth any more. He did not call me Francis or dad, it
was Geb. His voice chilled my whole being as it was
one I recognised from my past and not the recent
once loving present. Steven was now someone else
he uttered curses in our ancient tongue and I knew
that had he found the statue of the hawk first then
he too could have read the message.

 He must have been standing in the wadi as he let
off a few rounds in the direction from which we
had just come. The chase was on. Our man was a bit
distracted by the gunfire or simply blinded by the
flashes of the gun. More important was that I could
see him in that instant and he was not looking at us.
My ears were ringing with the noise of the fusillade
and I was hoping that held good for everyone. It
would buy me the chance I needed. I had to kill him
silently and not give our position away.
Incapacitation would not be sufficient as he would
be able to trap us at any time. He had drawn the
short straw and would pay with his life if it were
within my power to take it.
My hand closed around a large stone that had been
pressing into my side. Gently pulling it free and
realising that we only had one chance, I sprung up

in front of him striking at his head as I did so. The improvised weapon connected with a horrific crunch as his skull crumpled and I felt his blood spatter me. He sank to the ground with no further noise. Dragging his lifeless body to the depression I removed his dark jacket and an Uzi machine pistol with two magazines. I was beginning to look like an itinerant arms dealer but at least this killing machine was designed for in your face combat and could spit rounds better than the AK47.

Anna was speechless and just cowered there looking horrified at the blood glistening all over me. I pulled her to her feet and clamped my hand over her sweet mouth lest she scream. I did not feel much better myself; gory close combat killing is not easy for either party unless one is mad. I turned away and retched dryly as silently as I could.

The skirmish line had now passed us, we could continue our escape down the valley but we would still not be safe until these maniacs were disposed of. I knew that I had to stop them before they stopped us. I could not run away any more. I had been a great king once and perhaps would be again. As Geb I was a warrior. Malik my Prime Minister whom I had once loved as a son, had betrayed me once before and would desecrate my tomb should he find it. He would also use its contents to finance his evil plans.

I remembered the words on the disks; I did not
want the sands turned to glass with a Russian
bomb, if that was what the message had meant. I
did not want this done in the name of Allah or any
God. It was not right for evil to triumph over good.
It would not be what a peaceful or merciful God
would want anyhow.

Only I could stop this madman now. He had the
might of his evil employer from my past behind
him; he could cause more death and fear even if he
did not steal my treasure. He would cause death,
discontent and mayhem wherever he went.

Mubarak was right to be afraid of him.

It had worked before, would it work again? The
circumstances might be in my favour. I whispered
my plan to Anna as I concealed her amongst the
rocks.

After making it safe, I gave her my pistol for
reassurance. 'You must stay here absolutely still no
matter what. If I do not return, you must wait for
Khalid. I love you beyond life itself. If I die, I shall
wait for you.' I stifled any contrary reply with a kiss
and stoked her cheek feeling a tear as I left her
there, 'I love you too Francis', she whispered, as I
slipped away into the darkness.

My intention was to infiltrate the line at some point
and initiate a firefight. It was obvious that most of
my pursuers were untrained, cheap thieves and

malcontents, picked up to carry out Malik's wishes.
They would be afraid too, believing me armed and
dangerous. They knew I had taken the weapons
from the Toyota They would be expecting a bullet
out of the darkness and I would not disappoint
them.

Concealing Anna had taken about five minutes, so I
had a little distance to make up on the line. They
had not realised how far and fast we had travelled,
and so were looking further up the wadi. They were
not being exactly quiet as I stalked behind them
seeking cover from the sides, staying a few steps
behind in the deep shadows.

I joined the line at what I took to be its centre. I
could only guess but they were at the same
disadvantage as I, except they did not know I now
had a close combat automatic weapon and that I
was amongst them.

Wrapping the jacket around the barrel to blank the
muzzle-flash, and making sure it did not snag the
bolt or ejector, I aimed at a group to my right.
Scything down three or four with my first burst, I
turned left and sprayed fire at where I thought that
group would be, hitting some of them before they
hit the deck. I then dropped down to the ground,
rolling back as fast as I could.

For a moment there was silence, then the night was
torn by screams of pain and fear punctuated by the

crash and the stroboscopic flash of automatic gunfire from both right and left as they enfiladed themselves. The air over my head became populated with death. It was mayhem, more men started screaming and I was glad that they were dying in their own crossfire. I slipped away before my true position could be discovered relying upon the fact that they like me were deafened by the sound of gunfire and would not hear my retreat. I heard Malik shouting to cease-fire but there were too many nervous gun barrels for him to control. I guessed he had his head down too. It would stop when the bullets were expended. I estimated there might be six to seven killed or injured. It was a pity Malik was not amongst them. I was resolved now to kill him. It was the only way. Leaving the scene I could still hear sporadic fire and curses echoing off the Theban hills away behind me.

I reached where I believed I had hidden Anna. It was difficult to see any landmark but I risked a stage whisper in Italian, for only I would. 'Cara Mia, my dear' which was answered in like form by the frightened lady who had patiently awaited my return. She rose up and hugged me so tightly that I worried she might break my rib.

'Hey! Take it easy, remember that is where I was shot a week ago' She relaxed her hold and gripped my arm in relief. 'What happened Francis? I

thought you had been killed. There were so many
shots and screams. Oh Francis, when I heard
someone coming I was so afraid that you had been
killed; that I almost wanted to kill myself. When
you called to me in Italian, my heart filled with joy.
It could only have been you. I love you so.'
I knew I had to break this moment and said as
kindly as I could 'If we don't get out of here now
we will be dead. It won't be long before they will be
coming back to the truck ' True to my prediction,
we heard shouting and movement. I had to act fast.
I could not let them get away and continue their
activities. The consequences were too great.
Perhaps we could now take the truck? I vaguely
remembered its position relative to where I had
hidden Anna. We made our way silently into the
wadi and followed it further down to where I
assumed they had parked the truck. The moon had
moved in the heavens and we could not risk using a
light.
 Reaching the concealed vehicle took a little time
but in the dim light I noticed the bonnet was up.
They had immobilised the engine and were
advertising the fact; we were not going anywhere. I
was now so angry that I would kill anyone in my
way. I was extremely mad and had to restrain
myself from smashing the entire machine. Apart
from a waste of my strength, it would trap us all

together with the obvious result that Anna and I
would be dead at sun up. I must do something else.
There was no way I could wait in ambush, the Uzi
as good as it was, could only be used at close
quarter. The barrel was too short for accuracy; the
AK47 however was accurate over a greater distance
but we were outnumbered. It would be suicide to
attempt anything from here. They could get the
high ground and shoot both of us.   I felt around the
truck, perhaps we might find something
worthwhile. There were Jerricans held in racks
along the sides and rear. I loosened the tops of a
few to see if they held fuel. Those at the side did
I smashed a rear light plastic cover. Pulling the bulb
and its connecting socket out of the assembly still
attached by the cables, I broke the glass envelope
gently, trying not to break the filament. I could not
be sure that I had not, I could only pray. I undid the
top of one can that was tight between the side of the
truck and the side of the wadi and inserted the bulb
and wires as deep as I could into the aromatic fuel.
Screwing the cap back on
 I was aware that time was fast running out for us.
All my life I had been defusing bombs and now I
was just about to kill using one. It did strike me as
ironic that this was to be the way I wished to kill
my only son. I had no choice. Khalid had been in
the same situation regarding me earlier and had

trusted me enough to let me go to perform this final cruel murder. I would not get another chance without killing Anna and myself. It had to be this way too.

We used the dead mans jacket to sweep our tracks from around the truck just in case they used a torch to detect our visit and made our way as quietly and quickly up the side of the escarpment. I had to assist Anna to make the short climb as we were almost totally spent.

We then lay on our stomachs, panting with fear and exhaustion, looking down on the vehicle, which reflected a tiny moonbeam or two. It was just enough to see by but without any details being visible.

I heard a slight scraping noise and whispers as they checked to see if we had found the truck. I was glad they had reversed it into the defile as this might mask the fact I had booby-trapped the side.

Satisfied we had not been there, a voice said, 'Come on' and a bedraggled band slunk into sight.

Someone shone a torch on the engine and replaced what I assumed to be the rotor arm. We could see some men were helping comrades into the truck. Steven was strutting around madder than me. I knew his posture, his moods and his motive; it was a shame I had not known his soul.

Chap 32

I knew he was afraid now. It was all I could do not
to weep with the thought of what I had to let
happen. He got into the passenger's side after the
driver had unlocked the door, the inside light shone
on his face, which was a mask of utter evil. I felt my
blood run cold as I recalled the last thing I had seen
before he had killed me in my previous life. Geb
had been killed by his trusted advisor and so called
friend, his own son. The story was now complete.
History would be rewritten tonight.

The engine started and the truck moved out of the
defile, into the open desert. The headlights came
on, ripping through the darkness. I knew that if the
filament and wire were intact, it would be heating
up and vaporising the sloshing petrol. Soon it
would ignite it and.

A terrific explosion tore the darkness apart as the
contents of the can covered the whole truck with
flaming death. Men were thrown out as the vehicle
toppled on to the drivers' side. More cans exploded,
turning it into a hydrocarbon fed hell. I saw
individual fires move erratically around the desert
floor, they were devouring the flesh of living men
as they ran in an attempt to escape the clinging
flames. Their screams were interspersed by the
continuing detonations of the Jerricans. The orange

and yellow flames were being eclipsed by the thick black smoke from burning tyres.

I watched without feeling but not without objectivity. Here was I who had spent most of his life preventing such suffering; now able to inflict it when it suited me. I was not sure if this would work. Anna was horrified and lay beside me immobilised by what we were witnessing. One by one the sounds of agony ceased as the sparks of life were extinguished.

Soon it was silent except for the crackle of the burning tyres and human torches. The smell of hell wafted back to us where we lay along with the moaning of those trapped. I was sure Steven was among them. The explosion would surely bring Khalid along with help.

I felt the rage and elation of Geb. It was not like me to find pleasure in the pain of others. I knew this was the only way to finish off our enemy. Still I had to make sure, and so I now made my way down the wadi. It was easy now because of the illumination from the funeral pyre in front of me. I checked again that the Uzi and AK were combat ready and covered the last hundred metres or so with care. Stepping over the blackened corpses of several once human beings, I tentatively approached the cab sweeping the gun barrel to cover myself. Flames were beginning to feed on the seats and persons

trapped within. The heat was building as I saw
Steven half out of the window; his lower body
engulfed in flame. He called out to me in our
ancient tongue. 'Geb, my father, you have won. Kill
me, Kill me'
For a moment I was tempted to end his suffering
but my distant memory and the picture of the
burning man on my tomb alerted me not to have
compassion. If I was to release his Ka before the fire
did, he might take over some other innocent person
to continue our fight. 'No I have had enough. You
did not grant me mercy' I looked up towards Orion,
away from him and cried out 'By Ra our father, I
shall show no weakness this time'
'Kill him Francis, or I shall' I had not heard Anna
approach. And had assumed that she would still be
watching from our vantage point. Turning towards
her, and being in her line of fire I said ' It must end
here and now. Put the gun down Anna' She moved
around to take a shot, her hands were shaking with
the apprehension of what she intended to do. ' I
was his mother. He was my son once; you cannot
let him suffer. Move out of the way, I beg you.' I
stood; unmoving blocking her shot and said 'Anna
that is Steven my own son now and then. If we kill
him by any other way than fire, he will be able to
haunt us for all eternity for as Set he will live again.
He is Set and I am Horus. This battle has lasted

thousands of years and will destroy the world if we let him return. He must die by fire and by fire alone. His atoms must be scattered to the desert winds and not a part of him shall remain. That is what Yussef and the discs have told me. That is what I saw on the tomb'

Pointing at Steven, I now moved away, inviting her to kill him. It could not be long before the fire did anyway. He had passed out still cursing me. I was amazed by my own callousness as I shouted, 'If we give him a warriors death, it will be the end of our love' I saw her face register the meaning of my words. She would have to choose the past or the future.

Letting the pistol drop to her side, she turned away, not wishing to witness Steven burning like a wax dummy. The fire rose up and consumed him the crackling roar of its passage marked the release of his Ka to the underworld for all time. He would never return now. She looked terrified and I hid her face with my chest.

Her body shook with the sobs of grief and horror as the strain of the last few hours broke through. 'I unloaded it anyway,' I said, indicating the weapon. She turned back towards me; I could see the light from the fire behind me dancing on her beautiful face. Anna simply said, 'you knew all the time? And

yet you still loved me enough to know that I would
not defy you?'

I nodded and pulled her into my arms. The useless
pistol dropped at my feet. 'Yes Anna, fate brought
us back together again and I knew deep inside that
you would not betray me. You did not fail me then
or now. We shall be able to end all this without
hurting our love. I need your love to heal my
agony; I also need your counsel to help me survive
the conflict I feel inside. I need you more than ever
before to unlock our past, present and whatever
future we shall have. You must understand that it
was part of the eternal battle of good and evil. I
hope the sacrifice will be worth the personal
tragedy we shall have to bear. We are simply
puppets dancing on the strings of time.'

I knew that the grief of my loss and my
involvement in Steven's death would haunt the part
of me that would remain Francis Edwards for all
my life. I was not sure how Geb would cope with
me for the rest of his. Eternity is a long time.

She kissed me hard and putting our arms around
each other's waists, we walked towards the dawn. I
could hear the sound of engines bouncing down the
valley as Khalid and his entourage approached. It
could only be my giant friend coming to our rescue.
I would lead them back for poor Imir; or perhaps
they had found him already. I hoped that he had

not been discovered by Steven or his men and realised that Khalid would be relieved to find out that we had not been betrayed by one of his own countrymen.

My own relief at the end of this episode and my growing love for Anna, plus the fact that there was to be a more comprehensive reunion of the class of God knows when BC; began to tear the remains of my sanity almost to breaking point. I felt knowledge of things to come and things that had passed as Geb fluttered in and out of my present mood. The transformation was obviously going to take a while yet but I knew that it would only make me stronger and more able to love this enigmatic country that had started my journey through the millennia unto now.

The sky in front of us hung like a gigantic curtain with pinpoints of celestial light woven within its gradually lightening folds. I felt the heavens pull my ka back into the present and was aware of another external part of my soul that had been hiding beneath my conscience for a long time. I would come to rely on this in the future; I had no doubt about that. A flash of premonition told me that this was not over and that the past few days had been simply a beginning.

I shivered as this realization and the last vestiges of the long nights coldness washed over me. We

walked on like two zombies, deep within our
separate thoughts; for Anna too had been affected
by the raw cruelty of my nights work. I hoped that
she would not suffer further from the memory of it,
or blame me either for being able to kill my own
son.

Our shadows cast by the dying flames, danced in
front of us on the rocky sides of the wadi.

 The night was almost over. We would open the
tomb by the right entrance and set my Ka free. Its
beauty would show the world that when my
ancient people came to this planet we brought
progress. We did not bring hate and greed, envy or
dishonesty. They were here anyway, long before us.
What we would find there and the power it would
bring to those who held it, would be another story;
perhaps as protracted and dangerous as this one. I
would let fate and Geb guide me there.

I felt the warmth of Anna beside me.

'Come my queen let us live in peace'